AUGUST ORIGINS

ALAN LEE

For Sarah
For Always

I was neat, clean, shaved and sober, and I didn't care who knew it. I was everything the well-dressed private detective ought to be.
-Raymond Chandler, *The Big Sleep*

1

The first day at my new office, I sat in the swivel chair and glared at the oscillating fan and ignored emails beckoning from my laptop. Correspondence in this heat bordered on absurdity. It was late summer and temperatures kept touching triple digits. Perhaps I had moved into the new office too early; the air conditioning was noisier here than in my basement.

Like all professional and winsome investigators, I ruminated on the more important things in life. Such as, if Rooster Cogburn was real and alive today, what pistol would he carry? Maybe the third generation Peacemaker, Colt .45. But that gun had some glamor now, thanks in part to Rooster, so maybe a less flashy Smith & Wesson 19? Or would he carry a semi-automatic, like a Glock? I snorted. Rooster Cogburn would *not* carry a Glock.

These things needed to be considered.

Also, maybe I should get a bottle of scotch for the bookshelves. Would clients be put off without one?

My office was on Campbell Avenue, downtown Roanoke, Virginia. Second floor, above a bookstore and the restaurant Metro. From my window I could see an Orvis and a river of millennials on cellphones streaming to the local farmer's market. To purchase responsibly grown broccoli. Maybe some elite asparagus. To produce truly exquisite steel-cut urine. All paid for with Apple Pay, pure sorcery.

My building was 1920s classic revival and Beaux-Art, built before World War II. The stairs creaked and the central air-conditioning groaned but I'd moved with certainty that clients would rush the doors with bags of cash. And perhaps be a princess in distress.

Thirty minutes before lunch, the stairs creaked and snapped. A new client. I remained calm.

Sheriff Stackhouse entered. I recognized the sheriff from recent campaign posters. Approximately fifty years old. Brown hair showing the first streaks of silver. Excellent physique. Rumored to be a hard-ass. Pretty green eyes. She read the name on my door, "Mackenzie August."

"Sheriff. I notice you're not carrying bags of cash."

"I'm hoping you take Apple Pay," she said.

"I don't know how. But you may ogle my new office for free."

Sheriff Stackhouse wore tight khakis, which flared at her lace-up Kate Spades. Her white button-up shirt was tucked in, sleeves rolled up, collar flicked wide. Rumors were, she was enhanced surgically. I'd heard her described as good breeding wasted on public service.

The sheriff was followed by a man who resembled what a police detective should look like; thick, buzz cut, hairy forearms, snub nose, maybe forty-five. Vaguely resembled a Rottweiler. Not good breeding.

Two clients.

He threw me a nod.

"You look like your father," Sheriff Stackhouse told me.

"Except handsomer?"

"I haven't seen him recently. I don't recollect quite the same breadth of shoulders, though. You played football in college, yes?"

"With varying degrees of mediocrity."

Sheriff Stackhouse sat down on the chair placed opposite mine across the desk. She shifted to accommodate a pistol and badge clipped at the small of her back, and crossed her legs. "At Radford University? Their first team, if I recall."

Buzzcut snorted. "Never won a game." He poked through the stuff on my bookshelves. Probably looking for the scotch.

"In my defense," I said, "we were terrible."

"I remember reading about you in the papers," she said. "I'm glad you returned home."

"Good to be back."

"Do you have a few minutes to chat with Sergeant Sanders and me?"

"I do."

She held out her hand and Buzzcut placed an iPad into it. "I'd like to verify some information about you."

"Sounds exciting."

She powered on the tablet and ran her finger across the screen. "You were born and raised in Roanoke, Virginia. Played on Radford University's first football team and earned a dual degree in English and Criminal Justice. After graduation you moved to California and joined the Highway Patrol. Worked your way onto the Los Angeles police force. Was assigned to homicide. Promoted to detective. Got mixed up in the high-profile North murders. Took a leave of absence that became permanent. Briefly worked in a church before moving to South Hill, Virginia and teaching English for one year. Came home last year, couldn't land a teaching job, so you got your private detective license and contracted out to local law firms. How am I doing so far?"

"I was my apartment building's chess champion in California."

She returned to her iPad. "You fought in underground cage matches in Los Angeles. You were reprimanded multiple times while on the force for insubordination. And last year you shot your coworker."

Buzzcut sniffed, possibly with approval. "Shot the bastard twenty times."

"Am I still accurate?" she asked.

"Essentially. My coworker needed shooting. And try not to make me sound like a cliche."

"You come highly recommend by Brad Thompson Law in Salem.

He says your work is so good you're now in demand by other firms. The Los Angeles police captain told me I'd be a horse's ass if I don't hire you. And finally, you have a son named Kix."

"Last but paramount in importance."

She clicked off the iPad and returned it to Buzzcut. "I'm here to potentially offer you a job, Mr. August."

"Not interested in police work," I said.

"Good. I'm not interested in having you in my office."

"Rude."

"Roanoke has a gang problem. A significant one. You're aware of this?"

"Roanoke doesn't have gangs. Roanoke has illegal organized groups involved in territorial disputes."

She smiled. Kinda. "You're quoting me. From the article in the Times a few weeks ago. That's only bullshit I feed to the press. We have a gang problem."

"Oh dear."

"It stems primarily from narcotics. On the East Coast, cocaine and opiates such as heroin are smuggled in from South America, Mexico, and the Caribbean. Although there are many points of southern ingress, much of it is temporarily warehoused in Atlanta, awaiting distribution. But the drugs don't stay there. Unfortunately for us, Roanoke is the halfway point between Atlanta and New York City. Seven hours, each way. Billions' worth of drugs travel up and down Interstate 81, and Roanoke is a convenient meeting place."

Buzzcut Sergeant Sanders spoke up. "Roanoke's a staging area. A shit ton gets stashed here by the local gang."

"Bloods," I said.

"Yes. Crystal meth hasn't hit us yet, thank god. We've got our hands full as it is."

I placed my elbows on the table and steepled my fingers. "You've come to the right place. I'll take care of this gang problem."

She smiled again. Kinda. "Ha ha. It's a bit beyond one man."

I kept my fingers steepled, but I pointed one of them at Stackhouse and then at Detective Buzzcut. "Sheriff's office. And police. You represent different departments."

Stackhouse answered. "This is a joint endeavor. I've taken point but I'll collaborate with the chief of police."

"Lucky him."

"I agree," she said.

"I met the chief. Or what's left of him. We shook hands and I nearly killed him."

Buzzcut snorted and said, "I heard you was funny."

"*Were*."

"What?"

"*Were* funny. Or *are*," I corrected him. "Not *was*. I know it's complicated because *are* and *were* are both plural, but *you* does not take singular verbs."

"The hell you talking about?"

"Don't blame me, Sanders. It's the rules."

"You taught English, huh."

"Correct."

He held up a book found on my shelves. "This the Bible?"

"Better be. Else that's a terribly misleading cover."

"Why you got it in your office?" he asked.

"To pass the time between my affluent and attractive clients."

"You a Christian?"

"You got a problem with the Bible?"

Buzzcut said, "I'm a Christian. Went to an episcopal church when I was a kid."

"I don't know what Episcopal means."

"You go to church?"

"I do not."

He snorted. "Then you ain't a Christian, dope."

"Sanders, I'm entertaining the possibility you aren't the world's foremost expert on the subject."

"You say weird damn stuff, know that?"

"Boys, we've gotten off track. Sanders, close your mouth," Sheriff

Stackhouse said. "We're here because we need help. I have it on good authority a heavy hitter has recently moved to town."

"A heavy hitter."

"Gangs don't have strict hierarchies or leadership, per se, and in fact Roanoke is even less organized than most. The Bloods are subdivided into neighborhoods, like Lincoln Terrace. But the sets do recognize older and more powerful members. And apparently, the Roanoke Bloods has one. An important one. Nicknamed the General."

"Your sources are local and low-ranking gang members?"

"Correct. Incarcerated and willing to snitch for reduced prison sentence."

"How do I help?"

"By returning to the classroom. I'd like fresh eyes and ears inside Patrick Henry High School. I believe the General is active there."

"You want me to teach."

She nodded. "Yes. Tenth-grade English."

"This would interfere with my thriving private detective enterprise."

"Think of me as a ten-month client."

"You can't afford me."

She gave me a half smile, genuine this time, and shifted in her chair. "Sexy talk for a broke PI."

"That's economic profiling. I'm loaded."

"Yet you live with your father."

"The August boys stick together." I made a dignified fist for visual aid. "Solidarity."

"No interest in teaching?"

"The schools have resource officers. You don't need me."

"ROs wear uniforms. Hard to get fresh intel. You know this."

"I know this," I said.

"I need someone to listen in the tenth grade. That age is beginning to drive. Becoming more active in gangs. I want to identify the new OG."

"Original gangster. Roanoke's new big man."

"Yes. We know you can handle this because of your well-publicized heroics last year."

"I'll pass."

She sucked lightly on her pearlescent front teeth and tapped her index finger on the chair's armrest. "What is your hesitation? You were applying for jobs like this last year."

I shrugged, palms up, winsome smile.

"Now you're being an ass," she said.

"I know this."

"I've offended you. I said something uncouth, but I'm unsure what. I didn't realize men could be so prickly."

"Only us sensitive types."

"You do not strike me as a sensitive type."

"I'm not. But I pass."

She stood and moved to the door. "I'm not giving up on you yet. Okay?"

"You'll need to line up behind my many clients with bags of cash."

"Think about it. Please."

"Because you asked nicely."

Sergeant Sanders shot me with his finger and followed her out. He left the door open and the heat poured in.

2

The following morning my son Kix and I sat in the kitchen eating breakfast. He was almost two and concentrating for all he was worth on scooping bits of banana into his mouth using an adult spoon. He spurned baby spoons for reasons I hoped would become clear when he began speaking in full sentences.

He was a good-looking kid, no thanks to me. Got the big blue eyes, long lashes, and sudden smile from his mother. His biceps and deltoids, however, left a lot to be desired and he wasn't keen on curling reps with his firetruck. He took a draught of milk, slammed the cup, and gave me a grin.

Life was good.

We lived in the Grandin neighborhood. Big house on a big corner lot off Windsor Avenue. Big enough to have two staircases, sheer lunacy. A restored 1925 classic brick foursquare, so Timothy August said, with wraparound porch and interior craftsman woodwork. The yard was shaded with hundred-year-old pine, maple, and magnolia trees.

No mother, no cousins, no grandparents, just us August boys. When Timothy August found out we were moving to Roanoke, my old man put his trendy condo in Hunting Hills up for sale and bought this place on the condition we move in.

In my thirties, living with Dad. Just like I planned.

Kix requested more bananas. I told him to use his manners. He did, though he couldn't pronounce the "L" in please yet. I acquiesced anyway because I was a charitable and doting father.

Timothy August, my father, entered. Brown loafers, pressed chinos, blue sports coat. With three buttons, the saucy creature. He poured coffee from the carafe, sat, and snapped open a newspaper. "Morning, boys."

"No one reads newspapers anymore, Dad."

"Only those of us with class, son." He lowered the paper long enough to smile at Kix, who responded with sunshine. "Hello, grandson."

Kix pointed at his food and expressed concern. Dad agreed. I got more coffee.

"Busy day?" he asked.

"I'm thwarting an evil apartment building which is being sued by clients who have fallen on the stairs. The proprietor arranged an impressive cover-up but I am undaunted."

"One of Brad Thompson's assignments?"

"Indeed."

"Sheriff Stackhouse phoned last night."

"She ratted me out?"

He tilted his head down far enough to examine me over his stylish bifocals. "She told me about the job offer."

"You two go back?"

"Yes. We've both lived in Roanoke for the past twenty-odd years, so..."

"She's quite the smoke show."

"She's always been attractive, yes. But she's aging remarkably well. She's only four years younger than me. WDBJ 7 is running out of reasons to put her face on screen." He sipped at his coffee. "Will you accept her job offer?"

"Not sure."

"I told her you wouldn't."

"How'd you know?" I asked.

"Too many bosses."

"I dislike bosses."

He nodded and returned to the paper. "Which is odd. Because they always seem to enjoy you."

"I'm enjoyable. But I'd rather not report to a principal, vice principal, English supervisor, department chair, *and* sheriff."

"I figured."

"You didn't tell her, though," I said.

"That you dislike bosses? I did not. I felt no compulsion to divulge more information than necessary."

"Atta boy."

"Still," he said behind his paper. "Still. Seems a shame. That school needs good teachers. Which, according to your previous supervisors, you are. Switching gears, is your fight tonight?"

I nodded. "Coming to watch?"

"Absolutely not."

"Wimp."

"You're a violent man." He sighed. "Probably take after your maternal grandmother. But that doesn't necessitate my viewership. Shall I drive Kix to Roxanne's? I'm leaving in five."

"Nah. I need the jog."

Kix and I went outside. I strapped him into the jogging stroller, shoved his bag into the storage pouch, and tightened my laces.

All of Virginia seemed to be boiling but especially Roanoke, which rested in a wide valley that trapped moisture. I broke a sweat within a block and was soaked after five. Like running in a sauna. Wearing a thick robe. After a mile I could've probably slipped through prison bars. But the overhanging leaves were a deep rich green and almost worth it.

Kix loved Roxanne's. She stayed at home with her daughter Lucy, who was the same age as Kix. Roxanne's husband taught at Roanoke College.

On my return trip, sans stroller, an impressive unmarked squad car slowed beside me and kept pace. Dodge Charger, eighteen-inch performance tires, 340 horsepower. I did the math in my head and decided I couldn't outrun it. Maybe with fresh legs. I decelerated to a walk.

The driver's window buzzed down. Sheriff Stackhouse. "Give you a ride?"

"I'm disgusting."

"Just the way I like it. Hop in."

I did. She cranked the air. A manila envelope rested on the passenger seat with my name on it. Inside were papers and photographs of teenage girls lying dead on asphalt. I shuffled through, trying not to flinch. Five years of carnage in homicide hadn't completely inured me. "Local? Recent?"

"Three in the last twelve months. All Roanoke City. Know what they are?"

"Rites of passage. Especially violent." I glanced down the medical examiner's report. Raped, beaten, shot. Gang markings on the ankles.

"What do you think?" she asked.

"I think you need to crank the air-conditioning."

She hit a button on the dash and a greater volume of cold air rushed forth.

"I think your gang problem is getting worse," I said. "None of these girls are white. They make the news?"

"One of them. Barely. Two of them are undocumented illegals, so... You know." She shrugged, an angry motion. There was a note of steel in her voice I hadn't registered yesterday. "If they were white, it'd be a national story. How messed up is our planet."

"Rites of passage aren't usually this brutal. Not even in Los Angeles. You think it's the presence of this new General causing escalation?"

"Exactly. And I figured you out."

"Yikes."

"I asked you to be a narc. A professional squealer. And insulted you, in so doing. I apologize."

"Think nothing of it," I said.

"There are worse things than working undercover, though."

"Teachers do not work undercover. Which are you asking me to do?"

"I'm getting desperate, Mackenzie. Let me take another shot at you."

"Sure."

"I want you for ten months. After that, I'll quit molesting you. You never have to meet with me or Sergeant Sanders, unless you so desire. I'm after additional eyes and ears, not more meetings. We know the gangs have infrastructure within the school, but we don't know how they communicate. Despite all security measures, the schools are infested with drugs. Raids turn up stashes but few culprits. The gangs recruit soldiers within the halls, arrange hits, rumble between classes, you name it. We're making no progress, and those gang initiation murders scare the hell out of me. If I could get some intel on the structure and hierarchy..."

"The General could be identified."

"I'm worried about escalation, so I'm throwing myself at you. Find this guy. Whatever you want. You run the show, you set the terms."

"I enjoy Krispy Kreme doughnuts."

She smiled. "I will hand deliver them weekly."

"You show up even once at the school, I'm out."

"Understood. I was being funny. Like you."

"I have prior obligations, so I'll need additional days off."

"I can arrange that with school administration."

"No meetings. No hassles. I know your number. No reason to bother me."

"None." She was nodding.

"When does school start?"

"One week."

"Okay. You've got me for ten months."

3

A few months ago I overheard a couple guys at the gym talking about a local mixed martial arts club. They met twice a week after-hours in a local karate academy for sparring. No full-time professionals, but these were legitimate fighters coming from surrounding areas to train for events like Spartyka and Titans of the Cage. Many of them ranked top five in the state in various weight classes. So I joined and trained, twice a week.

Tonight was my first fight since California, over two years. Nate Silva was ranked second in Roanoke for heavyweight and fourth in Virginia, and I was going to be a snack between ranked matches. The dojo was crowded and I knew no one, but before the match a couple guys kneaded my shoulders and tightened my black sparring helmet.

"You fought before?" he shouted above the din.

"Not recently."

"You a big dude. So get him to the ground. He's nasty, amigo. Tough and strong."

Silva was across the mat. Shorter but thick with muscle. Snarled face, calloused from previous fights. Shaved head, eyes lidded like a snake's. I'd seen him practicing other nights; mean, vicious kicks, threw a hard left.

I pulled the thinly padded fight gloves tight. Three five-minute rounds. To win, score the most points or manage a submission move. The dojo maintained a standing gentlemen's agreement to not maim one's opponent. We met in the middle. Sweat trickled down his head. I tasted the familiar coppery adrenaline. The ref issued standard rules and we touched gloves. Back to our corners and the bell rang.

He led a feinting straight kick, but I didn't bite. It surprised him and jolted his rhythm. He was proud and expected a fifteen-second knockout. I shifted back, let his right hook pass, and I hit him with a short hard left. Should've dropped him but he moved like lightning. Instead of removing his nose, I caught him in the cheek. Bells rang in his eyes. Disoriented. Pop pop to his vulnerable nose. His eyes watered, and he shifted to protection. I chased for four minutes, peppering his defenses, but his superior footwork and quickness saved him.

Bell rang. I got water, firmly ahead in points. He sat down to recover. Murmurs of approval rippled among the onlookers.

Next round, and he came out aggressive. A fury of fist attacks. I could see why he was ranked fourth in the state. His hands landed hard and my arms and shoulders bruised. After a minute he saw an opening, stuck a foot behind my leg and forced us both to the mat. He landed on top and I lost my air. His mat work dwarfed mine and I spent three minutes avoiding submission. He snarled and spit and punched and kicked and wouldn't let me up, but I was concrete, and he couldn't break.

The bell rang and my helmet was torn off. Round over. I relaxed. But Silva raised up and drove the heel of his hand into my unprotected temple. Pow.

Stars, roaring black.

Outraged fighters bounded into the ring and hurled him back. He kicked and bit like a madman. I sat up, woozy. Lungs burning. Men I didn't know told me to follow their finger, brought water.

The refs announced, "Silva's disqualified. Judges are unanimous."

Silva swore and paced on the far side of the ring. I rolled my head and shook my limbs. No concussion.

I owed him. Wanted to bust his ass. I told the ref, "Let's finish it."

"You've won, big guy. No need."

I tugged my helmet back on and took water. "Had worse. Ready to go."

The ref walked away. Silva smirked from his corner. The crowd was conflicted. I thought to reassure them with a pithy comment but talking hurt.

The bell rang and he came on. As in the previous two rounds, he attacked. I assumed defense. Playing possum. As he closed I struck a jab that startled him, then hit a right-left combo. Dodged a weak counter, and lunged. Shoulder in his chest. My hands circled under his thighs and lifted. Textbook pile-drive. The air leaving his lungs was audible. I spun him and ground his face into the mat. He clawed and kicked, but my knee was in his back, forearm across neck.

"You're not getting up," I said.

He hissed.

"Surrender when you're ready, sweetheart."

The crowd chuckled and cheered. I could put him into a painful submission move but, alas, I am virtuous. He growled and squirmed until the bell. I released and he shoved me as he rose.

I won the points. Won two out of three rounds. And he'd been disqualified. Three out of three wasn't bad. Except I could barely move.

I WENT to Blue 5 for a beer on the way home. A trendy restaurant and bar with a modern blues theme, polished hardwood, muted lights, no live music tonight. I sat on a tall wooden chair at the busy bar with a view of the Washington Nationals game. We were up three against the Mets with two innings left.

Ooooooouch, everything hurt. My adrenaline high was wearing off.

The bartender came for my order. She was, perhaps, the most fetching person I'd ever seen in real life. Aphrodite herself. Under the hanging bulb, her hair was the color of sunlight, pinned up. Easy smile. White button-down and black slacks worn like evening wear.

Cool it, August. Never let 'em see you sweat.

"Oh my. What happened to you?"

"Walrus," I said.

She laughed. Yessir, old Mackenzie still got it. "You need a drink."

"I need a drink."

"You strike me as a beer guy."

"Got Stella Artois?"

"Only douchebags drink them," she said.

"Better make it two, then."

She shook her head and smiled. Such a sight I was nearly struck blind. Forcefully I turned full attention back to the game. I didn't come here to hit on bartenders.

Focus on the game.

Focus on baseball players. Gross, nasty baseball players.

She brought a draft, set it on a napkin, leaned her hip against the bar, and watched the game as she dried glasses.

"Bryce Harper."

"Yep," I agreed.

"I would marry that man just for his hair," she said.

"Me too."

"Except you're straight."

"Still. That was a long home run."

She said, "You're an imposing man. Why are you so big?"

"The good Lord and His infinite wisdom. Now shush. I'm watching the game."

"I don't shush. I can tell you're new because I'd remember that swollen sweaty face."

"It is neither swollen nor sweaty in perpetuity," I said. "Normally I'm gorgeous."

"Too bad. Kind of a good look. Did you move here recently?"

"Spent much of my life in Roanoke, southwest. Came back last year."

She said, "Where's your accent from?"

"Formative years spent in Louisiana."

She was called away by a patron down the bar. I did not watch her walk away.

Well. I did. But I'm not proud of it. The view was worth the self-loathing. Light on her feet, constant motion, good muscles.

Guy two seats down, already a little over-served, leaned my way. "I think Ronnie likes you."

"Is Ronnie what you call yourself? Because that's odd."

"What? No. Idiot. Her, the girl. She usually deflects conversation."

"Maybe because you refer to yourself in the third person as Ronnie," I said. "Big turnoff."

"What? You're being a asshole. I'm just saying."

"*An* asshole."

"What..."

"An asshole, not a asshole," I said helpfully.

"You weren't so big, I think I'd like to kick you in the teeth."

"Yeah, sorry. I'm a little punchy tonight. My apologies. Next round's on me, Ronnie."

"*Her* name's Ronnie, not mine," he said.

"Whatever your name is, you smell unfortunate."

He swore and left.

The bartender from Elysium returned a few minutes later and said, "You ran off Frank. A couple more whiskeys and he would've started singing."

"He said you have a boy's name. I pointed out that you can be any gender you want and we won't judge."

"You're a mess."

"But on the bright side, I'm sweaty."

"Did you look at my ass earlier?" she asked.

"Ahhh...no?"

"Because you should. A girl in my building believes she has better hamstrings than me, so I've been busting it. I need to prove her wrong. These things are important."

"Maybe I should be the judge of your contest," I offered.

"She was a gymnast but I was a dancer. Perhaps it's a tie. Where'd you go to high school?"

"Cave Spring," I said.

She speared olives three at a time. "We're rivals, I went to Franklin County. When'd you graduate?"

"We're not in the same decade."

"Never know. I'm old, but I take vitamins by the fistful."

I told her. She told me. Not old. I was two years her elder.

"You played football," she said.

"How'd you know."

Her eyes were a shade bluer than hazel. I think she actually glowed. I had a hard time maintaining her gaze, like my soul would catch fire. She shrugged and it looked good. "An indistinct suspicion."

Yeowza. Mackenzie, going off the rails. Gotta get out of here.

I said, "You don't look like a Franklin County girl. You're a little too...eye-catching."

"Mmm, spoken like a boy from Cave Spring. What's your name?"

"Mackenzie."

"Mackenzie what?"

"Sorry. Mackenzie, *ma'am*."

She grinned. "You're a mess, Mackenzie. You don't flirt like the other boys."

"I'm holding back. If I flexed you might drop whatever glass you were holding."

She left to fill a raft of drink orders. Ronnie didn't look like a bartender. More like an A-list celebrity here on a hidden camera show. She returned as I finished the beer.

"I *just* figured out who you are," she said.

"Knight? Shining armor?"

"I wish. You're the investigator who works with Brad. Usually you're less clammy."

"How do you know Brad Thompson?" I asked.

"I've been co-counsel with his wife. Twice. I've helped her with an immigration case. You and I were in the same courtroom three months ago."

"You practice law."

"I practice law like Giselle wears heels."

I raised my hands, palms up — huh? What? Who?

"I make law look good," she clarified. "I have my own firm."

"A lawyer moonlighting as a bartender."

"Similar professions. Taking money in exchange for false hope. Brad told me about you. He says you're excellent and you shot a teacher."

"Those two possibly do not belong within the same sentence." I slid money across the table. "Thank you for the drink, Ronnie."

"You're leaving."

"I know trouble when I see it."

"I'm the best kind of trouble, Mackenzie."

"Also I need a shower," I said.

"Badly."

4

Kix was asleep. After my shower, I lifted him from the crib and rocked him on the glider. He was wearing the type of onesie that had feet, but it was getting too small. He settled against me and his breathing deepened. Nothing like it.

Ronnie. Wish we hadn't met. She was in my head after only a few minutes. Shoulda turned and ran the moment I saw her. Bartenders used to be my type, and the source of pain. Had never met one who practiced law though.

I returned Kix and got a water. Dad was in his room with a lady friend, door closed, so I sat alone in a rocking chair on the front porch. Even eleven at night, there were walkers on the sidewalk. Safe neighborhood, and the humidity had lifted.

Going from a lot of sex to none is like being on a diet. I'd been stuck on none for two years, and every girl looked like chocolate cake. Shoulda cranked the temperature down on the shower. I went back inside, and instead of *faire l'amour* I got into bed with a book by Ursula Le Guin.

Not as good.

5

Patrick Henry High School was good to look at. Modern brick, circular atrium, and walls of windows made popular in the early 2000s. Inside was more glass, shiny flecked floor tiles, and lockers galore.

Two women sat behind the counter at the front office, busy with paperwork and their monitors. The woman on the left had short brown hair, a turtleneck despite the heat, and a necklace, which had clearly been made by her grandson. She glanced at me over her bifocals but did not stop typing. "Help you?"

"Mackenzie August, an appointment with Ms. Deere."

"She's ready for you." She hadn't stopped typing. Must be some kind of superhero. "Go on back through the hallway."

I obeyed.

Ms. Deere's office had a particle board desk, a window, two chairs, a particle board bookcase, and just enough room to turn around in. The woman herself looked forty, thin like a runner is thin, chin-length hair tucked behind her ears, and attractive in a severe fashion. "Mr. August?"

"Vice Principal Ms. Deere."

"Please have a seat." She nodded to the chair. Her fingers were laced over a newspaper flat on the desk.

Doesn't matter how old you get. Walking into the principal's office is never a good feeling.

I sat and tried to look innocent.

"I don't like it," she said.

"Can you be more specific?"

"I don't like you working here."

"Then don't hire me," I said.

"Unfortunately, Mr. August, that is not up to me."

"I knew I should have worn a tie."

Assistant Principal Deere cleared her throat and picked up the newspaper and read:

"'Local hero Mack August is at it again. The eighth-grade English teacher who discovered the recently deceased body of Mackenzie Allen and subsequently aided South Hill law enforcers in the arrest of a local drug dealer, and the discovery of a small stockpile of illegal narcotics, is making headlines once more. Last night, Mack August responded to the distressed telephone call of Emily Newman, August's coworker and the middle school's technology resource teacher. Before police could arrive, August interrupted what Emily Newman describes as the worst night of her life. Newman was working late when an unidentified individual broke into the school and attacked her. The assailant fired a small caliber handgun at August while he acted as a decoy, allowing Newman to escape in his car. The mysterious perpetrator, who is believed to be the killer of Mackenzie Allen and Jed David, escaped without injury.'"

She finished reading and re-clasped her hands, and frowned.

"Pretty good, right?" I said.

"I do not think it's funny." She tapped her finger on the newspaper. "A few days after this story was written, you got into a gunfight on school grounds and shot a man. Correct?"

"Correct."

"Killed him," she said.

"Mmhm."

"Three dead bodies, at least one of which you murdered."

"At the very minimum."

"You're acting like a child."

"And you're using shame to manipulate. Won't work. I'm an oak," I said.

"I do not want a gunfighter on this campus."

"What about a mild-mannered gun fighter?"

"Stop," she snapped and pointed her finger at me.

"Sorry."

"I should warn you, I'm taping this conversation," she said.

"Yikes. Maybe I should sit up straighter."

"This is a violent place, Mr. August. An underfunded and understaffed violent place. It's hard to persuade good teachers to work here, and those who do leave after two years. Half our students go home to nothing and come back the next day wondering if they'll get tangled up in a fight. Or worse. We're trying to educate them, they're trying to survive, the state is breathing down our necks to raise scores, and the Sheriff wants to conduct an operation in our halls by installing one of her thugs into a classroom."

I said nothing.

"Some of our students have done time, and quite a few others should have. I realize you're a big man. A really big man. But that will only make them want to challenge you. You're a threat to young men looking to prove themselves. And if word gets out about your motive for being here, you might as well walk around with a target on your back."

"How would word get out?"

"I have no idea." She met my look levelly.

"I taught in Mecklenburg County. At the time, it was the poorest county in Virginia," I said.

"So."

"So we both know scores are higher in affluent communities. The more money mom and dad have, the higher the scores. The less money, the lower the scores."

"Generally speaking, yes."

"And I was in the poorest county," I said.

"Okay."

"My students scored a ninety-four percent on their SOLs."

She didn't say anything for a moment but her eyebrow arched. Then, "Not bad."

"You'd be thrilled with an eighty-five most years."

"So you're a thug who can teach."

"Mild-mannered thug who can teach," I reminded her helpfully.

"Are you being financially compensated?"

"Not by the Sheriff. Standard teaching salary."

"Why? Tell me why. Why did you sign up for this?" she asked.

"A teacher affects eternity."

"Spare me the quotes."

"My son will be going to these schools. As you said, these are violent halls. I can help."

"You can." It wasn't exactly a question, but it wasn't a statement of faith either.

"I can."

"Sheriff Stackhouse told me about the powerful gang leader who moved to town recently."

"He's why I'm here. He and I need to talk."

"What will you do?" she asked.

"Cross that bridge when I come to it," I said.

"If you ever act like a cop instead of a teacher, Mr. August, I'm firing you on the spot. Understand?"

"This could be the beginning of a beautiful friendship."

6

I spent the week prepping. Planning. Girding my loins. Meeting fellow teachers. They thought I was amusing. And handsome, I'm sure, though no one mentioned it. I also tied up loose ends with various clients, informing them my time would soon be limited.

The night before school started, Timothy August and I sat on the porch playing a game of chess by citronella torchlight. We were straight from a movie about life in Georgia during the early 1910s — drinking lemonade on the front porch in our rocking chairs, listening to cicadas and complaining about the humidity. Our drinks were spiked with Patrón tequila and Dad had a Vegas Churchill clamped in his teeth. A baby monitor hissed softly on the windowsill.

I was winning. My opponent brought his queen out too early. Senile in his old age. He stewed.

My phone buzzed.

>> **Mackenzie August**

>> **I procured your number from Brad Thompson**

>> **To inform you...**

>> **I will allow you to take me out to dinner**

>> **Should you so desire.**

>> **You didn't come to my bar Friday night**

>> So I assume either you're cowardly or blind
>> Either way...
>> Consider this an act of charity.
>> I like Italian. And big sweaty men.
>> — Ronnie

"What are you grinning about?" Timothy August asked.

"I do not grin. And none of your business."

"That better be a girl. You haven't been out in...I cannot remember when."

"One does not cast pearls before swine."

"Is this girl swine?" he asked.

"No. A local attorney. Who also tends bar, and launched a thousand ships."

"Oh yes? Helen of Troy? Take her out. You must. I'll pay. One of my dreams is to come downstairs for breakfast and find a redhead wearing one of your shirts."

"It's your move, you weird gross old man."

"I just want to see you happy."

"Happiness is not necessarily something brought by a redhead," I said.

"In my experience she does."

"Are you happy?"

He shrugged. "Who's to say what's happiness."

"You've had a couple girls over recently. Not working?"

"Same girl, twice. She was...uninspiring."

"It's your move, you weird gross old man."

We finished the game. The good guys won. As we cleaned up, a car pulled into our driveway.

Dad glanced at his watch.

"Expecting company?"

"Everyone I know in Roanoke is on this porch or asleep in a crib."

The headlights extinguished, and a man got out. Shoes crunched on gravel. I finished my lemonade, the ice clinking, and rose.

The deadliest man I'd ever met stepped onto the porch. Manuel Martinez. Went by Manny. A former friend on the police force in

California. I hadn't seen him in two years. Normally shockingly handsome, now his eyes were sunken and his face was clammy.

We embraced and he pounded me on the back.

"Buenas noches, mi amigo."

"You too," he said.

"You smell awful."

"Mind if I crash here?" Manny asked.

"Spare bedroom's upstairs."

"Gracias. I drove here from LA. Straight through."

"Seems excessive."

"Because I'm loco, hombre. Thirty-five hours. Now, beauty sleep."

"Dad, this is my friend from Los Angeles PD. Manny, this is Timothy August," I said. They shook hands, and Manny went inside.

Dad watched him stagger upstairs.

"Do you trust that guy?"

"I do. And I have. With my life."

"Just like that?" he asked. "No questions asked, take the guest bedroom?"

"You'd prefer he share yours?"

"Absolutely not. But where does this trust come from? Some sort of brothers-in-arms code?"

"Called friendship, Timothy."

"But Kix is up there, and that *hombre* looks unstable. Tattoos everywhere."

"He had a very different upbringing than you. But relax. He was there the night Kix was born. And at my partner Richard's funeral. I trust him."

He said nothing.

"Besides," I said. "I've been thinking you'd look good with a few tattoos."

"Goodnight, son."

7

M anny did not sleep in the guest bedroom. I found him on my floor, with a pillow and no blanket. A big .357 peeked from under the pillow.

I knew the feeling.

The next morning he came down to breakfast and lowered himself gingerly into a chair. Manny was a good-looking dude. His waist was thin and his shoulders set far apart. Great cheekbones, so I heard. He needed a shave and shower.

"Mack," he croaked. "Can I crash here a couple days?"

"Long as you want."

He locked eyes with Kix. Kix regarded him, icily. "Holy shit," Manny said. "Your boy looks like Melynda."

"But with muscles? And the promise of future facial hair?"

"Sorry about sleeping on your floor."

"I care not where you sleep. What brings you?"

He shrugged.

"Took a job here."

"Surely you jest. What job?"

"I'm a US Deputy Marshal now," he said and got coffee. "Training ended last week. Five months."

"Wow."

"Sí."

"They'll let anybody in, these days," I said.

"Needed a break from homicide. Was becoming a desperado."

"Sergeant Bingham gave you a good recommendation?" I asked. "That guy hated you."

"Kinda. Un poco. He was going to transfer me, so instead I requested he recommend me to the Marshals."

"Por qué?" I asked. "Why transfer?"

"Usual stuff."

"You kept releasing the hot suspects?"

"People have such issues with sex. No comprendo. What are you doing now?"

"First day of teaching," I said.

"No joke? Certainly you're the baddest assed teacher in America."

"And we're about to be late." I cleaned Kix up and hoisted him. "Do me a favor. Go easy on my old man."

"Qué?"

"You're not white, and he scares easily," I said.

"My grandma was white."

"Oh thank goodness. We're saved."

～

ROXANNE OPENED the storm door as we walked up her steps. She was in slippers and sweats and glasses and no makeup.

"Hi Kix!" She held out her hands. Kix was unimpressed. "Today we're going to play with Play-Doh and puzzles and books!" Satisfied, Kix deigned it time to transfer out of my arms.

"You're good," I said.

"First day of school?" she asked. "Nervous?"

"Nah. I'm going to tear the arms off one kid per class and hit them with their own appendages. Establish dominance."

"Wow. I taught a couple years and just gave the students time-outs."

"Wuss."

"Have a good day!"

"Back around four. Bye Kix," I said, but he ignored me. Already playing with Roxanne's daughter.

"Hey," she called as I walked down her steps. "I want you to meet someone."

"No."

"No what?" she asked.

"No I don't want to be set up with your friend."

"She's great! You'll love her."

"Does she tend bar?"

"No."

"I'll be mean to her just to spite you."

She laughed on account of how funny I am.

A KID IS NOT SCARY.

The opinion of a student is not important. The collective opinion of twenty-five kids, however, is almost a physical force. New teachers think they will stand and deliver, and students will take notes and thank the teacher afterwards.

Hah.

Fifty percent of teachers quit within three years. Most can barely stand after the first day. Students don't realize how close they are to anarchy. The teacher's control is an illusion. It's not physical. Teachers give orders and hope the twenty-five teenagers don't rampage. Because there is little to stop them.

There is an old saying about teaching: don't smile until you're three months in. You smile, they pounce. Don't smile, always exercise control. You're the captain, the chief, the pack leader. Ten percent instruction, ninety percent psychology. Fifty percent brains, fifty percent nerves of steel. Raise your voice and you've already lost. Never let them see you sweat. Confidence and attitude. Stuff like that.

Here we go.

The school was polished bright and the air was sharp with optimism and fear. Veteran teachers joked from their doorways. Rookies focused on re-straightening their desks. A custodian pushed a wide mop down the hall and Ms. Deere hurried past, inspecting me doubtfully. I stopped by the office, signed in, and checked my mailbox. Copiers already ran full speed, hangdog students already sat in chairs waiting, and receptionists already droned into phones.

The teacher across from me, a happy guy as tall as he was round, passed back and forth in front of his door and preached encouragement to anyone who'd listen. His name was Reginald Willis, but we went by Reggie. This was his twenty-eighth year teaching.

"Repent, my brethren! For the heathen cherubs rattle our doors!" he called and earned a few laughs. "To arms! To arms! Our weapons be wisdom and wit, and our charges many. The state sends us savages but we'll make citizens of them yet. Mr. August, look'atcha. Big white man in the prime of life. There stands Mackenzie like the bull in a china shop. Are you scared?"

"I fear no man. Not even thou."

"Let me give you some free advice, young man." He waddled over. His bifocals perched on his nose, secured by a small chain which wrapped round his neck. "For me, my personal self? I treat 'em with respect."

"All they got is pride, Mr. Willis."

"All they got...well, now, go on, Mr. August. That's right. You're smarter than you look. All they got is pride, some of them, and we can't take that away. You and I, we take away their pride, you know what we got?"

"A cornered wild animal."

"A cornered wild animal. I like you, Mr. August. Don't look as though you belong, but you got more wits than most. Treat 'em with respect." He nodded to himself and waddled back.

I shared a homeroom class with another teacher for the first day. She was in my room and writing on the board.

"I hope you don't mind," she said. Her name was Ms. Bennett and this was her first year. Brown hair back in a ponytail, denim skirt, pink top. Her face reminded me of a puppy's. Her voice quavered as she spoke. She didn't know if she could control her students so she compensated by controlling what she could. Like names and dates on the board. She'd be terrified well into the semester. "Your face looks better. The bruises are gone. I still can't believe someone hit you."

"My face is elite."

"Did you kill the guy?"

I smiled. "No. Against the rules."

I stood by the door, arms crossed. A trophy case glinted across the hall. Fluorescent bulbs reflected off floor tiles. Posters with slogans like "You *Can* Learn" were attached to Ms. Bennett's door, adjacent to mine.

"I bet you're not scared," she said. "You're huge."

"I get nervous."

"Okay," she said, scurrying about. "Okay okay."

"Hey," I said and held out my fist. She bumped it. Tentatively. "You're going to be great. You're the best. Remember that. Captain of your classroom."

She nodded.

"Got it. Captain of my class. Be great. God I'm so scared."

Not a lot I could do for her. Sink or swim. The bell rang like an alarm going off in a bunker. Buses emptied. Doors flew open. Students barged.

The basketball players were taller than me, and I was tall. The football players were as big as me and I was big. Some seniors had scars. The girls were loud and full of disdain.

How did they see where they're going? Everyone stared at phones. Reginald Willis harangued them on the evils of cell phone usage, and the students loved it.

Tenth-grade students filtered into my room. Bennett and I made sure they knew where they were and where to go, pledged allegiance to the flag, participated in a moment of silence, listened to the principal's welcome speech, and sent them on their way. Time for first period. Bennett walked unsteadily to her door.

Always stay in the hall between classes, near the door. This was my hall and my classroom, not yours. Cut down on violence. Students coming down the hall gave me a wide berth, taking long looks at their schedule to make sure the scary guy was their teacher. They had to squeeze past me to enter. It's the little things in life that make me smile.

The bell rang. Class began. I closed the door with a bang.

"First things first," I said. "You're in Mr. August's tenth-grade English class. And you hit the jackpot. I'm the best. The best English teacher you're ever going to have. There was talk of giving me Teacher-of-the-Year award before school started. Understand?"

No immediate response. Wide eyes. Good.

"Yo, man, Mr. August. What kinda name is that? You know August Alsina, the rapper? August is a black name."

"What Jeriah has done wrong," I said, and floored him because I remembered his name from looking at pictures, "is he did not raise his hand and wait until called on. That will not fly in this class. What Jeriah did right is realize that I'm the best and I do not mind questions like that."

He grinned. A student's name is his or her favorite word in the English language. Use often. Jeriah Morgan sat near the back of the class. Hair cornrowed, pencil tucked behind his ear, name-brand clothing. Big, striking in appearance, an alpha male.

"Megan," I said. "Please hand out the class syllabus."

Megan, a cute little girl in tortoiseshell glasses, complied. She flitted about the room, dispensing paper like fairy dust.

Jeriah raised his hand and said, "Yo August, you like football?"

"Played in college."

"For real?"

"We'll talk after class, little man."

Laughter. The rest of the class was easy. The alpha had been dealt with. He tested me and deemed me worthy. The paths were a little straighter now and time passed quickly.

The bell rang after an hour. Jeriah stayed.

"Mr. August, you looking at the the starting running back on varsity."

"As a sophomore? Thought you looked quick."

"Damn right. Gotta come watch a game sometime."

"Guaranteed," I said.

"Aight. Catch you tomorrow." He strutted away.

I repeated the same drill twice more that day. After carefully scrutinizing all my students, I concluded the gang general was not one of them. No violence. No outbursts. Just reading and writing, which I enjoyed. Before leaving, I texted Ronnie.

You have the wrong number. No cowards or blind people here. Just us handsome douchebags.

Her reply was quick.

>> I like big sweaty guys...

>> AND handsome douchebags. ;)

>> And I haven't been out in a long time.

I've decided to ask you out. For the free booze.

And your hair. I liked your hair.

>> Anything else you liked?

I plead the Fifth.

>> When and where?

I'll let you know.

>> I wait. Breathlessly.

She sent a selfie. Winking and smiling.

My heart nearly stopped. Hard to look that good. She wore a trim navy blue jacket. Dainty gold necklace. And sex appeal.

On the way out, I stuck my head in Ms. Bennett's room.

"How'd it go?" I asked.

She sat at her desk, staring out the window.

"I'm still here. I guess."

"Good. Tomorrow, someone steps out of line, make an example of him. Kick him out immediately."

She nodded vacantly.

Reginald Willis's voice was caroming from a distant hallway. "We have overcome! We shall prevail. This is only the first trial of many, my brethren."

I was almost to the back door when Nate Silva walked in. The

Nate Silva from our fight. He wore brilliant white Nikes, baggy Levis, and a tight black T-shirt. Head shaved recently, narrowed eyes, serpentine in appearance. Two kids followed him. His hands balled into fists.

"You."

"Silva. What a delightful surprise," I said. He blocked the door. I stepped aside to wait.

"Teacher?" he scoffed.

"That's right, Nate the Ain't. You got whooped by a teacher. How embarrassing."

"In a real fight, there are no rules. No judges." He was close to my face, hissing. He smelled of powerful cologne. "And you'd lose."

"How do you know?" I asked.

"Because I'd beat your ass."

"Oh gosh."

"You get that?"

"Oh jeez. That sounds terrible. But our faces are a little too close. Right? Because I'm thinking of licking you."

"Won't fight you here, funny man."

He's right — I'm funny.

"Master Silva?" one of the students asked. "What should we do?"

Silva glared at me another moment. I tried to look scared. Then the storm passed. "Some other time, teacher."

"Bye, Master Nate," I said. He went deeper into the school. I got to my car, thankful Ms. Deere hadn't seen the interaction. She'd skin me.

Question was, why did Silva have students following him around and calling him Master?

8

The week passed in a flash. I phoned parents twice for behavior problems, and got voice mail both times. Out of a deep sense of tradition, I visited the school cafeteria on corndog nugget day. And on tater tot day. And once for delicious strawberry milk. I wore the same khakis and blue polo two days in a row and no one commented, but I did laundry that night any way. Ms. Bennet hung tough, still alive. Reginald Willis carried on from his soapbox. No more Silva sightings.

Friday morning at breakfast, the August boys ate to the music of Manny's hammer in the basement.

"What's he doing now?"

"Putting in new stair railing," Dad said. "He's churning through the entire handyman list."

"Hispanics. Taking all our jobs."

"Speaking of, when does his start? At the marshal's office?"

"Monday," I said.

"Shame. Cheap labor."

Manny hadn't moved out. His stuff sat in our spare bedroom, but he slept on my floor. Pistol at the ready.

I had a date tomorrow evening with Ronnie. That thought kept me warm all the way to school. That and the summer heat. Temperatures would reach ninety-nine today. Too hot for clouds. I parked in the teacher's lot. My car still bore bullet holes from an encounter a year earlier which, oddly enough, occurred in a school parking lot. To date, no women had swooned over the vehicular scars, and that struck me as unusual.

Between second and third period, I witnessed a felony. Drug distribution. A light-skinned black kid with a red backpack went into the men's communal restroom. From my door, I had a view straight down the restroom's hallway entrance. Red Backpack greeting another kid, executed an elegant handshake, and made the swap. Drugs for cash. Not hard to spot, because they did their best to look innocent. Truly innocent people never care about looking innocent.

Red Backpack continued down the hallway. Reginald Willis patted him on the shoulder without looking at him. "Run along, children, for idle hands are the devil's workshop! Keep those eyes inside your head, Mr. Kirk! Hurry on, young women. Look'atcha, dressed up for these jokers."

The drug purchaser came into my room. White kid named Trevor. He walked to a chair in the back corner, sat, and looked at no one. Stared out the window. Drugs in his pocket or maybe backpack.

What to do, what to do, so many options. All of them fun.

But I did nothing. Not yet. I was after bigger fish.

For thirty minutes I taught *Fahrenheit 451* and symbolism until the lunch bell, at which the students filed out and charged the cafeteria. Leaving their backpacks.

Here fishy fishy.

I checked Trevor's backpack. No drugs. He had a pocket knife, which was against school policy, but so what. I could have the school's resource officers frisk Trevor but, again, so what. Probably over half the school population would try weed before graduation, and chances were good that's what Trevor had. No need to hurl pebbles at a tsunami.

Red Backpack, however, interested me. Distribution is different than consumption.

At the end of the day, I packed up but paused at the door.

Maybe...?

I followed a hunch and sat down at Trevor's desk. Looked around. He was in the corner, near the wall of windows. No immediate hiding spots. I scrutinized the desktop surface and struck gold.

Students were leaving notes for each other by writing in pencil on the desk. Tiny letters in the corner.

Dice 4 sale.

$$??

20 per

Tmrw?

Dice was slang for cocaine. Twenty dollars per rock, fairly standard. Some of it was smudged out, but inexpertly so. Written by students in the same class or alternating classes, which would indicate a two-day written conversation between Trevor and another student later in the day.

Perhaps Trevor was distributing after all. Getting the dice from Red Backpack and filtering it out through his classes?

I checked the windowsills. Nearby books. Wall vent. Under the desk's writing surface. Nothing. Finally I ran my hands under the chair. Bingo. Hidden beneath, out of sight, was a cardboard tube duck-taped to the seat. Felt like a toilet paper roll. Empty.

The delivery system? Red Backpack gives it to Trevor, and Trevor hides it so he won't get busted? Or leaves it here for his friend to retrieve in a later class? They could leave both money and cocaine under the chair. Simple and effective.

I guess the drug community wasn't using Apple Pay yet.

∼

I WENT to the football game that night. Patrick Henry played Glen Allen High, and was winning 21-0 at the half.

There's something immediate and powerful about a football

game. Like injecting pure America into your veins, in all its glory and sin. Bright lights. Screaming fans. Proud parents. Rampant teenage insecurities. Pounding drums.

Manny came with me. He was such an attractive man, handsome to the point of beautiful, that teachers and students I didn't know came up to chat with me. And then organically transitioned to him. Two middle school boys thought he was famed soccer hero Cristiano Ronaldo.

"Good grief, amigo," he said when we had a moment of quiet. "I can't tell, these are high school girls or runway models?"

"Every girl looks good these days. Magazines, access to cheap stylish clothes, hair straighteners, and dieting. I find it sad."

"How do you keep pure thoughts?"

"Because they're kids and I'm not gross."

"You a better man than me."

"Agreed," I said.

"Should be a dress code."

"Is at school. Else the boys would never accomplish a thing."

"Ah, young love."

"Ain't love, you silly Spaniard."

"I was referring to that lovely señorita by the fence." He nodded toward a collection of girls near the end zone.

"She's a senior. Probably not eighteen. Maybe you should stare straight upwards."

"I'm no teacher," he said. "And if she's eighteen, I can look."

"You're thirty."

"No harm looking."

"Eh." I waffled my hand.

"You're a Puritan."

"There he is." I shouted over the crowd's roar. Red Backpack had wandered into view. Next to the bleachers, hanging with a crowd.

"Want me to solicit some delicious snow, señor?"

"Nah. I'm playing the long game. Plus, you are suspicious in appearance. He'd make you as a cop."

"Bust that ass, and you can return to investigative work."

"That's what I'm doing now," I said.

"Don't look it. You are standing still, hombre."

"My ways are mysterious. Besides, he's not the one I'm after."

"Whatever you say."

"And don't forget it."

9

R onnie lived at the Roanoke River House, two miles from Chateau d'August. The River House was a historic brick building modernized into industrial apartments for urban debutantes, and situated beside the river and the Roanoke Greenway.

I picked her up at seven. She got in and crossed her legs before I could even open my car door.

Her fingers slid between mine.

"I hold hands on the first date," she said.

She smiled. Spectacularly.

Mackenzie August, defender of liberty and tough guy extraordinaire, had trouble breathing for a moment. She wore a red cold-shoulder blouse with crocheted neck, jean shorts, and sandals with heels. It was not an immodest outfit. And yet looking at her felt scandalous.

"Let's get out of town. Head toward Bent Mountain."

"Bent Mountain Bistro," I said.

"That's the one. Wanna?"

"By all means."

"You're too big for an Accord, Mackenzie. How tall are you?" she asked.

"Not sure. Do you know how much you weigh?"

She laughed. "You're a naughty evil man."

I pushed through the gears and we motored southwest toward Floyd. Her hand stayed on mine and I didn't crash, a minor miracle. Brambleton Road wound up the side of Bent Mountain, giving us the best view in Roanoke.

The bistro's floors were wood and so were the table and stools. She ordered roasted chicken fettuccini, and I had the poor mountain spaghetti. Beers for both of us.

She had a way of speaking that bordered on laughter. Like we were in on a private joke.

"I did research on you," she said.

"A worthwhile endeavor."

"You worked the North murders in Los Angeles."

"That was me. And my partner," I said. "And eventually everyone else."

"I followed that news story religiously," she said.

"Lot less fun from the inside."

"I wanted to prosecute. I'd just gotten out of law school."

"Lucky. I was getting yelled at by my suspects, and the victims' families, and my supervisor, and the mayor. And reporters."

She waved for another drink and asked for a martini. I got water this time. Her food was half gone and she pushed the rest my way.

She said, "The guy you shot last year? I read he kidnapped your son."

"Indeed he had. Which is why he died so messily."

"Because I have a trained intellect and a graduate degree, I was able to deduce another fact about you; you have a son."

"Wow. You're good."

"Is that why you don't go out much?" she asked.

"Big part. He's one of those needy toddlers who requires supervision. Why don't you?"

"A lot of complicated reasons. Primarily, I'm boring."

"A woman will lie about anything," I said. "You don't strike me as boring."

"That's a sexist quote. And possibly true. Like I said, I'm complicated. A disaster."

"A single dad living with his father isn't?"

She laughed, and I imagine an angel got its wings. "Fair. You're a mess too. But your dark secret is only rated PG. I've got three doozies."

"Three secrets? Heavens. Maybe you'd better walk home."

She winked. "You won't survive me to find out what they are."

"On which date do you reveal you're a vampire?"

"The tenth. But by then I'll be watching sad movies on Netflix and eating ice cream alone. Listen, Mackenzie. This can't get serious. I'm not looking for a soul mate or anything. I was lonely, you looked lonely and handsome, so I got your number. That's it, okay? Two lonely people out to dinner."

"At the very minimum, I insist on a second date. Positively insist. I didn't even do my hair tonight."

Her fingers found mine again. "Yes. A second date. I'm still lonely. Do you cook?"

"I do."

"You may cook me dinner at your earlier convenience."

"Earliest?"

"Like I said, you're handsome."

The check was brought. I paid. She left cash for a tip.

I held the car door for her. She lingered a moment, close under my chin, those big bluish hazel eyes shining with the parking lot lamp, and then ducked into my car. She was tall for a girl, which meant just my size.

Whoa, regroup, Mackenzie. Stop staring. You're just standing there with the door open.

On the way home, she said, "I majored in nursing at first. Can you picture me in nursing scrubs?"

"Gladly. Why'd you quit?"

"My father made me. And the scrubs got too heavy, if that makes sense. Wasn't for me. Did you major in law enforcement?"

"And English. Double major," I said.

"A football player who can read? Bet you were a dreamboat on campus," she said.

"I barely made it out alive. And a cute blonde law student who can mix drinks? That would not be an unpopular combination."

"So I'm cute?"

"Was speaking hypothetically," I said.

"Nope. You can't take it back. I'm cute."

I thought of other places we could go, and rattled off several. Bob Dylan was in town. Or we could listen to the band at her restaurant. Or ice cream. Or whatever. It was only nine.

She wanted to go home. But she didn't look happy about it. She fell quiet.

At the River House she said, "Thank you, Mackenzie. This was nice."

"My view was better than yours."

"I can't invite you in," she said.

"Understood. I wasn't expecting an invite."

"Would you like to fool around in the car? I'm flexible."

I laughed.

"What a perfect laugh," she said. "Very masculine and also happy. But I was teasing. You cannot have me in the car."

"Good. Because I'm not into girls who fool around in cars on first dates."

"Why on earth not? Isn't that exactly what you'd be into?"

"Those girls have issues I can't cope with."

"Guess you'll have to take me out on a second."

"Only as an act of charity."

She smiled. Because I'm hilarious.

"I can't figure you out, Mackenzie. Good-looking guy. Good repu-tation. Mixed martial arts fighter, so you've got the dangerous bad boy thing. A little rough around the edges. But you don't date much. You didn't get drunk. No dirty jokes. No leering. Haven't felt me up. You seem so...serious."

"I'm not serious. More like determined."

"Why?"

"I want to do life right."

"Who is to say what's the right way?" she asked.

"Not me. I hit bottom, so now I'm doing the opposite of what I used to do. That's it."

"It's not about morals?"

"More like simple survival. Morals implies I know the right and wrong ways to act, which puts me in position to judge others. I'd rather not have the responsibility."

Her eyes were still big. She was leaning toward me but it wasn't suggestive. She was lost in thought. The air between us felt thin, like a vacuum. My advances would not be unwelcome. I got out and opened her door. She stepped onto the sidewalk.

"You're really not going to attempt?" she asked. "To get your way upstairs?"

"I'm patient. You look worth waiting for."

She flushed red, and I almost did too.

I said, "I'll call you."

She winked.

"Soon. I'm not so patient."

She disappeared through the door.

10

Monday. Second week of school. Only thirty-five more to go. Holy moly, that's a long time.

The second period bell rang, and I was ready. Because I'm an opportunist. The hallway surged with students. Red Backpack sauntered my way and went into the bathroom. This time he disappeared from view and emerged a minute later. He passed me and I dropped a heavy box into his hands. It was such a shock to him that he almost dropped it and bolted.

"You look strong," I said. "Help me carry that to the office?" I had a similar box in my hands.

"Say what?" he said.

"I can't carry both. You're the strongest kid I saw. The office is right there."

"Oh. Aight man. Sure." But Red Backpack wasn't happy.

We walked around Reginald Willis, who from his doorway extolled the virtues of meticulous grooming. We got to the office and Backpack was about to set the box by the entrance. Instead I bumped him through the door and said, "Put it on the counter. Thanks."

He did so, looking pained. Both the secretaries glanced up at us.

"Thanks...what's your name?" I said. I clapped him on the

shoulder and held him still a moment, so the office got a long look at him.

"Eddie, man."

"Thanks Eddie."

Eddie Red Backpack left in a hurry. I watched him a moment.

I removed the boxes and looked at the two women behind the counter. They looked back.

I smiled. A big smile. And was surprised it didn't set off the fire alarm.

"I need to know the name of that young gentleman. Do either of you know?"

"No."

"No."

"He must be new," said the lady in a turtleneck and ugly necklace.

"He's not new, else I'd recognize him," said her cohort. "I handle registration."

"So," I said. "You don't recognize him. But he's not new. Hmm."

"How odd."

Turtleneck frowned. "I'm not sure he goes here."

"Ah hah."

"What?" she asked.

"A clue."

Blank faces.

"Are you not impressed?"

They went back to work on their monitors. Probably too overwhelmed to express admiration.

AFTER MANY FAILED attempts and curse words, I finally remembered the passwords to my social media accounts. A girl I dated set them up for me a few years ago in California, and I'd neglected them.

Now I used their search features to learn more about Trevor, the kid in my class who purchased cocaine. Seemed like a normal guy. Pictures of him at Smith Mountain Lake. Of him with a girl in an

American-flag bikini. Of him at a concert. Nothing which hinted at major drug use or distribution.

In reality, Trevor was small potatoes. The system was full of Trevors and busting them didn't do a lot of good. Eddie Backpack was probably small potatoes too, but Trevor even more so because he was further removed from the supply. After this was over, though, Trevor and I would have a long chat.

～

I COLLECTED Kix from Roxanne's after school. He was asleep so I drove to the Greenway at Wasena Park, put him in his stroller, changed shoes, and walked all the way from the ballfields to Mill Mountain.

The Greenway meandered east to west for miles, and I moved through several distinct neighborhoods by the time I passed Carilion Hospital. Temperatures were in the eighties with a faint breeze, and the path was clotted. We navigated through joggers in active wear, strolling families, and irksome bicyclists. Kix woke up in time to point out nearby dogs.

On our return trip we stopped at the Green Goat, only a stone's throw from Ronnie's apartment building. The Goat was trendy and popular, but our wait wasn't long. The hostess was equally charmed by my son and my rugged good looks. We got a table and ordered pizza. Kix fussed. He thought pizza was too bourgeoisie. The Nationals were about to throw the first pitch on a television over the bar.

"Mr. August. What's up, man."

Jeriah Morgan was here. The varsity running back with a big mouth in my first class. He wore a purple and gold letter jacket, despite the heat. He came over and shook hands and met Kix.

"Mr. August, man, I didn't know you had a kid."

"I've only mentioned him a dozen times in class," I said.

"Ah. Well. I don't really pay attention. It's cool. Do you live around here?"

"Not far. You just get off practice?"

"Weight lifting only today. Done quick. Mr. August, this is my old man, Marcus."

He indicated the man coming our way. Jeriah's father was my height, which is hard. Gleaming shaved head, strong hands, long fingers. Dressed in jeans and a sports coat. He wore a silver Tag Heuer watch that matched his silver buttons. I felt sophomoric in my sneakers. Dang it.

His voice was Darth Vader deep.

"The fabled Mr. August. I've heard about you. And not only from Jeriah."

"Lies. Although you can see I'm almost as handsome as the rumors."

"Funny, is what I heard."

I knew it.

I made an attempt at modesty.

"Won't you come join us?" He indicated their table, at which sat a woman. The woman, whom I assumed was his wife, was shockingly pretty. Halle Berry pretty but with better makeup.

"Thank you, but my son Kix is upset we aren't eating at Frankie Rowlands, and he'd be a terrible dinner companion. His language tonight is filthy. I'll take a rain check."

He chuckled. "This gorgeous young man here? Never. Frankie Rowlands is high end for a little guy."

"He loves their pineapple martinis."

"Don't we all. Isn't raising a son the peak of life? My greatest achievement."

"Mine can't walk yet. Jury's still out."

"Raising boys is hard. It takes a village. Some days, makes me furious."

"The father is always a Republican toward his son," I said.

"And the mother is always the Democrat," he finished. "I quote that line to my wife. Robert Frost."

"We're soooo smart."

"Sure you won't join us? Good company is hard to find."

"Next time. My son might not last until the pizza arrives," I said.

"I appreciate your work at the high school. I know you're busy beyond the classroom and I'll be keeping an eye on you. You're a good man."

We shook hands again and he went back to his table. I sat down.

"Did you hear that, Kix? I'm a good man."

Kix fussed.

MANNY WAS in the living room. I put Kix down for the evening and joined him. He sat in the leather reading chair with his feet on the ottoman. Beer in his left fist, television remote in his right. He still wore his blue deputy marshal shirt. *Looney Tunes* was on the television.

I sat on the other chair.

"First day of work."

"Yep," he said. He held up thumb and forefinger. "Got a caseload this big. Grande. Virginia not so good at tracking wanted felons."

"We're still tired from fighting the British."

"All these criminals, amigo. Lightweights. Not like Los Angeles."

"Catch any?" I asked.

"One. Nasty woman. Tried to bite me."

"Who can blame her."

"Call Ronnie?"

"No," I said.

"Why not?"

"I'm not sure, Manny. I'm not sure."

"I looked her up. One hot mamita."

"I haven't seen the online photos, but assume she's better in person," I said.

"So what's wrong?"

"I like her. That's what's wrong."

"Ay dios mío."

"I think she's not in a place where she can like me back," I said. "Hard to believe, isn't it."

"You white people."

"I'm happy. And she's not the kind of girl you invite into your life without it causing waves. I dislike waves."

"You aren't scared of being hurt," he said. "You are scared of wasting time. Of losing focus. This girl, maybe she wastes your time."

"Well put."

"Maybe you need to have sex, hombre."

"You can't talk like that while Bugs Bunny is on screen. It's weird," I said.

"Think Ronnie needs sex too?"

"I didn't ask."

"Maybe," he said.

"Maybe. But do I want to? With her?"

"Yes."

"Yes. Yes I do," I agreed.

"But you aren't. I know. I know you."

"You know nothing."

"Unless you got drunk or high, back in the city, you had this nobility. Couldn't relax, you know? Couldn't have fun."

"Think about our friends, Manny. Our friends in Los Angeles. All our friends had fun."

"Sí. All our amigos are divorced and broke. But they were stupid, Mack."

"And we are not?"

"You are not," he said.

"What happened over there, Manny? Why'd you move here? Why the gun at night?"

He drank his beer. Stared beyond the screen at memories. Took his time answering. "One too many meth houses. Too many bodies. You know? One too many victims."

"You got people after you?"

"Only nightmares."

11

I took Tuesday off. It was too early in the school year for a sick day, but the school administration had been prepped for my absences. I was in hot pursuit of justice and the American way.

I wanted to follow Eddie Red Backpack. I had a hunch he wasn't a student at Patrick Henry, but the campus was so big and the student population so diverse he could slip in and out with ease. I'd only seen him before first lunch, so most likely he spent time in the cafeteria and then split. Otherwise he'd get caught in the hallways.

Arriving at nine, I parked my car in the teachers' lot behind the main building. I had Dunkin' Donuts coffee and Krispy Kremes and I listened to *Tell Me More* on NPR. So invigorating I nearly fell asleep.

While I waited, I texted Ronnie.

When shall I make you dinner?

>> **Three days, Mackenzie.**

>> **It's been three days since our date.**

>> **I'm the kind of girl you text later that night**

>> **I considered issuing you a subpoena**

I am playing hard to get.

>> **It's working. =)**

>> **Saturday? Your place?**

Saturday? That was forever. My thumb held steady over the phone screen, waiting for wit and inspiration to strike. Any minute now...

>> **All my other nights are booked. =(**

Saturday it is. 7pm.

Steaks? Chicken? Burgers?

Tacos? Salmon?

>> **Chicken!**

>> **I'm going to shop for a new outfit**

>> **If you're lucky, I'll send you pics.**

Objection. Leading the witness.

>> **Ha ha!**

I almost missed Silva. Master Nate Silva, my sparring partner. He parked in a black Toyota Tacoma, lifted high on hydraulics, and strutted inside wearing the same white Nikes and baggy Levis.

Note to self — find out why the heck Silva keeps showing up at a high school.

Eddie Red Backpack slipped out of the woods south of campus three minutes before the bell rang. Students emerged and he filtered in immediately. Lost in the crowd.

The woods. Interesting. Had to give him credit. He was a smooth operator.

I pulled up Google Maps. A stealthy reconnaissance of his journey home would be close to impossible. The woodland area adjacent to the campus was not small. He could park his car at fifty different points and walk here, or maybe he lived nearby.

I waited. And waited. And waited.

And thought about Ronnie's new outfit.

And debated Dak Prescott's chances of initial success without the Dallas Cowboys offensive line.

And tried to make sense of predestination.

And hoped Kix would start using more words soon.

And thought about Ronnie some more.

Eddie Red Backpack reappeared after second lunch. He exited through the rear doors and vanished into the trees. Gone, just like that. I charted his path from a few final glimpses, gave him a five-minute head start, and then followed.

He'd gone straight up the rise, so I did too. A small beaten trail wound higher through the pine and maple and poplar. It was a hot day but the shade was good. Squirrels scampered below and robins tweeted above.

Eddie might turn out to be nothing. Only a small-time peddler. If so I'd turn him over to the authorities, or maybe handle him myself. But there was also the chance he served a significantly higher authority, and he was as good a lead as I had so far.

Soon I found myself on Murray Run, a greenway curving through Woodlawn Park. Interesting. I wiped the sweat from my eyes and opened up Google Maps again and traced the greenway both directions. If I followed it another half mile, I'd eventually walk onto the big Shenandoah Life Insurance parking lot on the far side of Wood-lawn. An ideal place to park.

"Ah hah," I said.

12

The Salem Red Sox played the Lynchburg Hillcats that night. Timothy August's financial advisor had a private luxury box which was offered up for our use periodically. We sat in the shade and ate hot pretzels and drank cold beer from big plastic cups.

Most widowers who work as elementary school principals do not require financial advisors. Dad, however, had been married to a very successful realtor with a big life insurance policy. He also owned various rental properties. As with most ball games, he brought a portion of his school's staff to the game, and our private box was full of teachers cutting loose. Dad never dipped his pen into company ink, but tonight's cast was mostly unmarried young women. For my benefit.

Manny was a big hit. He tried keeping a scoresheet for tonight's game, but that required concentration and focus, two things soon wrested away by a determined kindergarten teacher named Alexa. Manny politely entertained the entire group until Alexa took the scoresheet away and requested he teach her. A professional move.

Kix was...somewhere. Upon my arrival, he'd been taken by women who referred to themselves as his aunts. I sat at the front, watched the game, made small talk with people I didn't know about life inside a school, and kept score. Nothing better than live sports. Somehow, even the colors are more intense. Almost photoshopped.

Three of my students were sitting behind home plate. Joshua, Zach, and CJ. Zach and CJ were in my last class together, and I had Joshua second period. I didn't realize they knew one another. They didn't even glance at the field, so absorbed were they with their phones and laughter. That was a good age. Fun and friends mattered most.

On my phone, I pulled up Trevor's social media pages again and scanned through his list of friends. The three knuckleheads below were absent. Trevor had lost his innocence sometime, voluntarily or forcefully; either way he was now in the drug community. Joshua, Zach, and CJ still existed in the innocent glow of halcyon days. I hoped.

Between innings I got another beer and verified Kix was alive. He was, though sleep beckoned. We could last one more inning, perhaps, so I seized the day and got a hotdog.

Timothy August sat next to me. He was still dressed for work, though his collar was loosened. "What's better than this."

"Not much."

"We should do it more often. I don't know why we don't," he said.

"Because this box is expensive."

"I don't mind sitting below, in the stands."

"With the peasants?" I gasped.

"Remind me, who was the player we saw last year? He plays in Boston now."

"Either Xander Bogaerts or Mookie Betts. The guy at second base is Yoan Moncada, signed out of Cuba. He inked a deal worth thirty-one million dollars, and he'll be in the bigs soon." I pointed Yoan Moncada out, the player chatting in the outfield at the moment.

"That kid has got some powerful glutes, doesn't he." Dad shook his head, a wistful gleam in his eye. "All that money. Sitting in Salem. What a waste."

"Most of these guys have second jobs to pay the bills."

"Not Yoan."

"Not Yoan," I agreed.

"Have you talked with Julie Coleman? She's our guidance counselor. Red tank top, drinking white wine."

"I have," I said.

"And?"

"No way. Bad ankles."

"What a twisted individual you are, son. Look at your friend, Manny, and how well he's going with Alex." He jerked his thumb over his shoulder at the happy couple.

"Alexa."

"Whatever."

"Alexa has better ankles," I said.

"You're joking about the ankles so I'll shut up. I know it. And I will. Shall I take Kix home? So you can stay longer?"

"I read somewhere that both The Rock and Tom Brady go to bed at eight thirty. So maybe I will too."

"Those two gentlemen are already married, I believe."

"Because women are drawn to men with early bedtimes, perhaps?"

He sighed and shook his head.

I hoped Kix would be a more rational son than I was.

13

Jeriah Morgan was running his mouth Wednesday morning. His buddy on the football team sat two chairs in front of him, too far for whispering, but today they chatted while I waxed eloquently forth on the perils of weak essay conclusions.

"Jeriah. Kevin. Hush."

Kevin, big guy with sunken eyes, said, "What?"

"I'm teaching. You're being rude to me. And to your fellow classmates."

"No one tells me hush who ain't my granny."

"I beg your pardon, Kevin, and I'm greatly distressed to hear I've used a word of which you disapprove. Oh no. I retract my hush and instead request you zip it."

"This is bullshit. I'm a grown man."

The classroom fell quiet. There was a hint of danger on the air.

"I can't say hush but you can say bullshit?" I said. "Seems unlikely."

"This class is a joke. Such bullshit."

"Kevin, step into the hall."

"Nah, I'm good."

Jeriah, his buddy the instigator, laughed. "Kevin, don't be a dick, go in the hall."

Wow. Language. Well, one battle at a time.

"Hallway, Kevin."

"Fuck you, Teach."

Kevin stood up. Tall kid, starting safety on the JV team. His Jordans were two years old.

"Going to the hall?" I asked.

"How 'bout you make me."

"Oh Kevin. Oh no. Such a bad decision. Your poor granny."

"You talk. All you do is talk talk talk. Maybe I kick your ass." Kevin was walking toward me. "Be worth the suspension."

Megan, the cute little girl near the door, was about to hyperventilate. "Mr. August, should I go get the principal?"

"No thank you, Megan. There's still time for Kevin to make a good decision."

"But—"

"Watch, Megan. Kevin's going to do the right thing. And then we'll all laugh and hug."

I was wrong. Kevin got into my face and threw a punch.

Who throws punches at teachers?

I threw a lazy forearm to block it.

"Okay, Kevin. Done? Now go into the hall."

He wasn't done. He shoved me with all his strength. And missed. I twisted and he staggered off balance into the whiteboard. His face smudged some of the dry-erase marker.

"Now you're done, I bet. Go into the hall. There's still time to be cool."

"Kevin!" Jeriah called. "What are you doing, bro! Listen to the man! They gon' lock you up!"

Another punch. Another miss. Like fighting in slow motion.

"Megan," I said. "Would you open the hallway door?"

She jumped to obey, nearly losing her glasses.

"Last chance, Kevin. Attacking teachers is a good way to end up in handcuffs. Go nicely into the hallway or you will be forced."

Kevin was embarrassed now. This would be talked about for days and he'd be the butt of jokes. He was dark in the face, breathing hard, and he came in a rush. Tackle the teacher, save his reputation. I bopped him on the nose, which brought him up short. It hurt. I got his arm and twisted it behind his back. Made him stand straight, on his toes, and I walked him through the door. Poor Kevin thought his arm was about to break.

"Now Megan. You may fetch a principal."

LOW AND BEHOLD there was another incident later in the day. Big fight in the hallway. A black kid and a white kid. White kid had a rebel flag T-shirt on and was screaming, "Nigger!" A crowd formed, with that electric energy only bloodthirsty mobs produce.

Reginald Willis tried to push through but without much energy. "Move aside, now, youths, move aside. No sir, put'cha phone away!"

I debated letting the white kid get destroyed by the larger student, until Ms. Bennett ran into the hall. She tried to break up the fight but got slammed into a locker.

Whoops. Partially my fault.

Most combatants want the fight to end. They want someone to break it up. Not these two. Rabid dogs.

I got my arm around the white guy's neck, nearly a choke hold, and hauled him backwards.

"Stay back," I told the other kid. "Understand? This fight's over."

He did not understand. The big guy came on.

I used my free hand. Grabbed him by the throat and slammed him hard into the locker. Pinned him there. A kid in each hand.

"Fight's over. Understand?"

Both students had flowing oxygen, but only just. A panicky feeling. Gets their attention.

He nodded.

The crowd of amazed onlookers parted. I hauled Rebel Flag to the office, out of which poured administrators and the resource officer.

"I'll handle the white supremacist," I told Ms. Deere, whose olive dress was ill-suited for fights. "You check on Ms. Bennett."

MANNY CAME home in time for supper. I was kneading ground beef and blue cheese crumbles into burger patties.

"Buenas tardes, guapos," he said, and ruffled Kix's hair. Or the fuzz Kix called hair. "I tailed your boy Eddie. Your suspicions were correct; he parks at the Shenandoah Insurance lot."

"I'm so smart I scare myself."

"Eddie left the lot and went to Cave Spring High."

"A second high school? Two in one day? Industrious young man. I like that about him."

"But he's pushing drugs."

"I didn't say I liked everything."

Kix threw cereal at me.

"Cave Spring has a wooded area adjacent to campus, same as Patrick Henry," I said.

"Correct."

"Eddie use it to cover his approach and retreat?"

"He did. You're so smart you scare me," Manny said.

"Muy intelligente. Eddie has a pattern. Where'd he go after that?"

"The mall. Want me to pick him up tomorrow?" he asked.

I was thickly coating my patties with salt and pepper.

"No. I'm going to follow him home one day soon. You want a burger?"

"Hell yes I want a burger."

"Language," I said. "Sometimes Kix repeats stuff."

Kix glared furiously at Manny and slammed his milk.

14

Principals have the difficult task of evaluating teacher performance. Only a maniac would base a teacher's effectiveness on test scores alone, so one solution is in-class evaluations.

A couple times a year a principal will observe the teacher. Principal wants to see lesson plans, engaging instruction, on-task students, SOLs written on the board, blah blah.

Assistant Principal Deere marched into my room during first period. She was dressed in a brown pantsuit that didn't hide the fact she took care of herself. This was very early in the year to monitor; we hadn't settled into a routine yet, and usually teachers get a warning as a professional courtesy. No such luck for me. Ms. Deere was out for blood. She sat at my desk and began flipping through my lesson plan book.

Lesser men would tremble.

Someone in the back, Jeriah I assumed, snickered.

"Mr. August's busted."

I told the class, "After you finish with your writing journal, open up to your notes section."

"Ugh, why?" Jeriah demanded. He was sprawled out, his feet almost touching the desks on either side. His boy Kevin wouldn't be back for a while.

"Raise your hand before you speak," I said. "And to answer your question, I said so. We're going to practice conclusions."

"Man, this class sucks," he grumbled.

But he was wrong. Most students loved this class. I knew for a fact Ms. Deere was getting good reports.

Hah.

I put a list of topics on the board and set the students to work on creating conclusions. As they wrote, I leaned down to Jeriah.

"You will stop talking in my class, otherwise your coach will no longer be able to play you during games because of suspensions."

He didn't say anything. The adjacent students listened.

"You will succeed in this class. And you will not disrupt it."

He knew I was serious. One benefit of my fight with Kevin — the students thought I was a badass. Crazy as hell, I'd heard.

If students realize you're bluffing and that you're afraid to pull the proverbial trigger, they'll walk all over you. They knew I didn't bluff. Tough love.

Ms. Bennett (who'd suffered a mild concussion) was new and she was afraid to follow through with threats. They ganged up on her, made the class wild and her life miserable. I encouraged her to "shoot" the leader by sending him to the office for a minor offense. Shoot the leader and his posse quiets, like Wyatt Earp. With detentions instead of pistols. But she couldn't yet.

The collective opinion of a classroom was a physical force. And she worried about upsetting them. Hard to blame her, but she'd be exhausted by October.

We discussed the class's conclusions. We brainstormed improvements. I engaged in elite Socratic questioning. Then we opened up our *Fahrenheit 451* novels.

Ten minutes before class ended, Ms. Deere snapped my lesson book closed and walked out.

"Are you in trouble?" Megan asked.

"Probably. I keep parking in her designated parking spot."

"Do you really?" Her eyes were wide behind the tortoiseshell glasses.

"No. And my lesson plans are perfect. She's mad because I'm so great."

Chuckles around the class. I'm hilarious.

"She's kinda fine, right?" Jeriah said. His hand was raised. "I mean, for an old lady."

"Jeriah," I scolded. But I didn't correct him.

AT THE END of the day, I stuck my head into Ms. Deere's office.

"Those lesson plans. Elite, right?" I said.

Her head was in her hands and she stared vacantly at her desk.

"I must admit. I was impressed," Ms. Deere sighed.

"Long day?"

"Yes. And I still have a mountain of work."

"I hope you're realizing that my classroom is in good hands. That I'm not simply a gorgeous thug. That I actually can teach."

She smiled.

"No one said you're gorgeous."

"I did."

"Yours is the only classroom in which a student has attacked a teacher."

"Kevin was high. And unprovoked. Mostly."

"Uh huh. I hope it doesn't happen again. And videos are circulating of you choking two students in the hallway."

"I am a legend."

"You certainly are. But the good kind? I'm unconvinced," she said.

"What purpose does Nate Silva serve here at Patrick Henry?"

She stared at me blankly.

"Who?"

"Nate Silva. Wears a tight t-shirt. Shaved head. Hispanic. Tattoos on biceps."

"Oh yes. Students call him Master Silva. He mentors at-risk students, and also runs some sort of karate studio. Tae kwon do, maybe? It's all Greek to me. He's been here a year. Is he part of your investigation?"

"I'm still in a fact-finding phase. Only curious how Silva fit in," I said.

"When he's here, he meets with students in detention. We've never had problems before."

"I'm sure he's a swell guy."

"Have a good day, Mr. August."

THAT NIGHT, Manny, Timothy August, and I sat on our front porch. We could hear live music from a festival in Grandin.

Kix had been tired and told me in clear words, "No song. Night night. Love you."

Well then. I should be Father of the Year.

Manny, Timothy, and I each had a beer to beat the heat and we were trying to remember our first beer. Manny had been nine when his mother began sharing.

Dad thought he was seventeen, but he told us, "It was different back then. We used to smoke at school, for Pete's sake."

"Mack?"

"I don't remember. I didn't like beer until mid-twenties. I snuck a pack of cigarettes, once."

"You did?" Dad asked. "When?"

"Backyard. Kept them behind the shed."

"I've failed as a father."

"Probably. Maybe there's still hope."

"So hot here," Manny said. "The air is thick."

"No humidity in Los Angeles."

"Not like this."

"However, the worst is only in July and August," Dad said. "Other than that, it's very pleasant. The humidity should dissipate soon."

We heard heels coming down the sidewalk. Sexiest sound in the world.

Dad looked up. "That will be Sue."

Sue was a divorced bank manager who ran by our house in tiny shorts every night, and she'd eventually made her way onto the porch. She laughed at Dad's jokes and touched his shoulder and one thing led to another. I debated informing her she was ten years too young for him, but she didn't seem to mind.

"Sue. From two nights ago?" Manny asked.

"No." Dad cleared his throat. "That was Karen."

"I have so many moms," I said.

"Señor August, you collect women," Manny said.

"I do not collect women. But. Don't mention Karen." He stood up to greet Sue. Her hair was up and she wore jeans with her heels. A good look. She threw us a perky wave and they went inside.

"So gross," I said.

"Love is not gross."

"Someone played a dirty joke on you, Manny. Told you the wrong definition of love when you were growing up."

"Maybe she is the one, yes?"

"Good ol' mom."

Manny's hand was wrapped with an ice bag. US Deputy Marshals were professional hunters. Charged with the apprehension of wanted individuals. When Manny got bored, he didn't use his gun. He egged them into a fistfight, like today, and never lost but sometimes bruised his knuckles.

Manny'd make a better gangster than law enforcer. He liked to fight. Was a crack shot, the best I'd ever seen. Was not above taking bribes or bending the law or killing suspects instead of apprehending.

And he still slept on my floor and watched cartoons. Not many gangsters do that.

We sat on the porch and drank our beer and thought thoughts.

Our silence was broken by Stevie. An eight-year-old kid who lived three houses down, we'd see him on his bike most days. Tonight, however, his face was streaked with sweat and his eyes were wide, like he'd seen a monster. No shirt, and his little chest heaved.

He darted onto our porch.

"Mr. August," he panted. "Can I stay with you?"

"Something wrong, Stevie?"

"Mr. Earl. He mad."

"What happened?" I asked.

"I broke a plate. He don't like it I break stuff."

"Is Earl your grandfather?"

He shook his head.

"Foster parent."

"Ah. I'd always wondered."

"Please? He's coming."

"Wait inside."

He darted through the screen door.

The monster came out of the shadows and into our porch light.

I'd met Earl our first week in the house. Quiet man in his sixties. Buzz cut, beard going gray, living on a railroad pension. He wore a stained white T-shirt and Dickies. No shoes.

"Mack," he grunted. "You seen my boy?"

Maintaining his balance appeared to be a challenge.

Manny and I shared a look. This was an unexpected turn of events. Several ways we could handle this. The fear in Stevie's eyes made me mad.

"Evening, Mr. Earl," I said.

"Evening."

"You look sick? Are you sick?"

"Ain't sick. Lookin' for my boy."

"You've been drinking."

"You ain't seen Stevie? Saw him running this way. Give him here."

I stood up and descended the porch steps.

"Why is a little eight-year-old kid terrified of you?" I asked.

"S'way they outta be."

"You smell like a garbage can, Mr. Earl. Go home. And sleep. Stevie can stay here for a while."

"The hell he can."

"I'd like to talk with Stevie, anyway."

"I'mma call police," he barked.

I put my arm around his shoulder. Locked him in place, my face near his. He stilled.

"Good idea, Mr. Earl. Let's call the police. Because I'll make sure they know you're drunk in public. And the kid in your care is afraid of you. And we'll ask both of you a lot of questions. Maybe, just maybe, you end up in jail tonight."

He didn't say anything.

"Go home, Earl. Go home and sober up. Right now. Stevie can spend the night here. You understand?"

I walked him to the edge of my lawn and released him.

He didn't turn. Didn't look back. Shuffled home.

I came back to my rocking chair and debated a second beer. Manny was on his second. I'm way tougher than him.

Stevie's silhouette hovered beyond the screen door.

"He gone?"

"Yes. Has he ever hit you, Stevie?"

"No."

"You sure?" I asked.

"Yessir. He get mad, but. Never hit me. Throws stuff sometimes."

"Just you and him?"

"I got an older foster brother. He's out a lot," Stevie said.

"You and the foster brother get along?"

"Sure. He looks after me some."

Stevie was staring at Manny. Even kids appreciated the depth of Manny's handsomeness. Mine must be more subtle.

"There's juice in the fridge," I said. "Get some, if you want."

"Okay!" He darted to the kitchen.

Manny stood and drained the bottle.

"Stevie and me, we'll go to his house. Get a change of clothes and his backpack," Manny said. "Back in five minutos."

"He can sleep in the guest bedroom, seeing how you never do. You going to rough Earl up?"

"Nah. Flash my badge, though, he gets tough on me," he said. "Arriba, Stevie!"

15

Saturday. Finally, sweet Saturday.

Ronnie came over at six. I met her on the lawn. She wore slim jeans and a silky pink top which tied at the neck.

"An asymmetric hem," I said. "Very trendy."

Her hand slid into mine. "You're a boy. You're not supposed to notice the clothes, but rather the girl under them."

"I can admire simultaneously."

"Then get started."

"Yowza."

She laughed, that magical sound I'd been hearing in my sleep.

"Much better. I got the shirt at Punch. You know it?"

"I do not," I said.

"Good. I prefer men with zero knowledge of posh boutiques. Your house is unbelievable. I'm so impressed. You do the edging? Do you know the names of these flowers?"

"Yes and yes. It's almost fall, so we've missed the highlights."

She pulled me to the side of the house so she could see the yard, her heels aerating my lawn.

"Mackenzie, this house is far too big for you."

"I'm a big guy. I'm not even flexing."

"Still. This is, what, four bedrooms? Five?"

"Not just me here."

As if on cue, my father came through the front door, adjusting his cuffs.

"Mack, I gotta run. Kix is in his chair. Wow, hello sun goddess, you must be Ronnie."

"I am." She shook his hand. "You two have the same eyes. Mackenzie's father?"

"Indeed. I'm Timothy, and very pleased to meet you. Stay as long as you like, the rest of your life even."

She laughed, and Dad was charmed. "I should have packed more."

"Shoo, Father. Shoo," I said. "You'll scare the pretty lady."

He got into his Lexus and winked. His tires crunched gravel as he left.

"He told me I should stay as long as I like," Ronnie said. "Does he...does he live here?"

"He does. Weird, I know. He insisted. That's why the house is so big."

I got to the front porch. She was still on the lawn, inspecting the house. She appeared befuddled.

"You *want* to live with your father?" Ronnie asked.

"I've spooked you. I can tell, I'm a detective."

"No no. It's not that. I'm unaccustomed to functional families. Or at least, families choosing to live together. I'd never live with my father volitionally."

"Don't get along?"

"No, we do. For the most part. Still." She half grinned. "It's complicated."

"Speaking of, come meet the cutest one."

Ronnie ooh'ed and aah'ed over the front porch and came inside. I knew she didn't glow. Or I was pretty sure she didn't. But every room she entered got brighter.

She saw Kix and gasped. "Holy fuck, Mackenzie. That's your son?"

"This is Kix."

His blue eyes were trained on her. In quiet approval.

She descended and scooped him up. No protest from the boy. I knew the feeling.

"Ohmygosh. I'm in love. At first sight. Head over heels. I've never seen such a gorgeous baby."

I had chicken thighs tenderizing, with an array of spices. I wrapped asparagus with lemon in aluminum foil, and squeezed the rest of the lemon into a pitcher of strawberry mojitos. I poured a glass and set it beside her, but she was busy letting Kix touch her face and vice versa. She was so happy she wiped tears from her eyes.

The Big Green Egg hit peak temperature, so I laid on the chicken, asparagus boat, and skewers of pineapple.

Ronnie came onto the back porch with me, Kix in her arms.

"So this is Casa d'August? The three of you beautiful men living together. In harmony. I swear, Mackenzie, this could be a show on HGTV and I'd watch every second."

"Yikes, you need to get a social life."

"I have no social life. You know what I'd call your HGTV show? Testosterone in August. Or maybe, Muscles and Pretty Eyes. Girls would eat this stuff up."

"Timothy August is quite the socialite. He'd be the star."

"He's a handsome guy, for sure. For his age? I'd fool around with that grandpa."

"You have already overstayed your welcome, you hussy."

She laughed. Again.

"This house even *smells* masculine. Polished wood. Leather couches. Cooking chicken. You're wearing cologne, and so was Timothy. And this little guy." She closed her eyes and smelled the top of Kix's head. "Perfect. Just like a little guy should. Baby powder and lotion and that indefinable quality."

"You like manly aromas, then you'll love our untidy bathroom."

"I'm serious, Mackenzie. Bring all your dates here. This is great. If I wasn't in complete possession of myself, I'd be aroused."

Manny came down the kitchen steps and stuck his head out the rear door. He was fresh from the shower. Thick black hair slightly wavy and damp.

"Adiós Mackenzie. I'm going to play pool. At some place called Awful Arthurs." He smiled at Ronnie. "Hi. You two have a good evening." And he left.

Ronnie waited until she heard his car start.

"That guy lives here too," she said flatly. "Doesn't he."

"I'm afraid so. Is this going to further upset your equilibrium?"

"Are you kidding me, Mackenzie? What is this, a house of male strippers? This is a joke. Has to be."

"His name's Manny. My friend from Los Angeles. Took a job at the local marshal's office."

"That guy is so pretty he's almost a woman."

"He'll be delighted to hear it. Shall we eat?"

Two hours later Kix was in his crib, singing. Ronnie and I sat on the front porch, his monitor cradled in her hands. Her chair almost touched mine and her feet rested in my lap. Citronella candles burned.

The night was warm but not sticky.

"Where is his mother?" Ronnie asked.

"It's a long story."

"I've had two mojitos, which were excellent by the way and I'm a professional drink mixer, and your food was delicious, and you smell divine and your arms look good in that shirt. I'll listen to anything you have to say."

"His mother is dead."

"That's awfully sad. But not a very long story. Were you married?" she asked.

"She was married to my partner, Richard. We worked homicide together."

"In Los Angeles. Is Kix your biological son?"

"They couldn't conceive, so I donated," I said.

"Smart girl. Those are some upper echelon genes."

"Richard died right before Kix was due. Murdered on duty. Crushed us all. Then there were complications during delivery, and Kix's mother never recovered."

"That's awful," Ronnie said.

"I ended up with Kix. Easy case, especially with the blood work evidence. No one else requested custody."

"And you left LA soon after."

I nodded.

"Got the hell out of Dodge."

Time wound on until nearly nine with a dreamlike quality. Kix's song was replaced by heavy breathing.

A kid rode past on a bicycle. Too late for that, but we had effective street lamps.

"All good, Stevie?" I called.

"Yeah, Mr. August, we good." Stevie chimed the bell on his handlebars and disappeared down the block.

"Who is that?"

"Neighborhood kid. Bad home situation. I'm keeping an eye on him."

"Of course you are."

"I'm basically the Pope."

She retracted her feet from my lap, stood, and she stretched.It was quite a sight and worth the price of admission, which had been dinner. She lowered to sit on the porch steps and patted the wooden slats beside her.

"Counsel requests the defendant for a private conference," she said.

"What?"

"Get closer to me."

I obeyed. We sat on the porch together, shoulders touching.

She smiled and I kissed her. We met in the middle. It'd been a while and I'd forgotten the sudden rush, the intense frissons radiating from contact.

She backed away long enough to ask, "When are the other hand-some members of this house of ill repute getting home?"

"If they show up now, I'll shoot them in the ass. But I'm not sure when they're coming back."

"You better kiss me until they do."

Which I did.

TIMOTHY AUGUST RETURNED AT TEN. Far too soon. Against my better judgement, I did not shoot him.

I walked Ronnie to her car.

"Brunch tomorrow?" she asked. "You can bring Kix."

"We're going to church tomorrow morning."

"You go to church?"

"Not usually," I said. "Trying to start."

"Why?"

"I believe it."

"Believe it," she repeated. "Believe what?"

"God. Genesis, a higher power, Jesus, Peter, the church. All that stuff."

"Me too. So?"

"If it's true then it's important. For me, at least."

"Does this mean you're never inviting me to spend the night?" Ronnie asked. She tilted her head up at me, and her eyes were wide and inviting.

"You want to have a sleepover? Sure, you don't mind the couch."

"Who said anything about sleeping, Mackenzie."

"You lawyers have such potty mouths."

"I'm not usually into romance, but tonight was romantic as hell."

"I noticed. Nothing escapes me, I have a degree in law enforcement."

"You're a romantic, aren't you," she said.

"I think so."

"I can tell. That's the only reason I'm not pushing you into my car to give you a goodnight present. I'd hate to sully the hopeless romantic."

"I'm not that romantic. Push away."

"I will allow you to retain your virtue," she said, through a dazzling provocative smile, "for one night more. But after tonight, I'm fair game."

I made a show of checking my watch.

"Only one more hour until tomorrow. Stick around. Virtue is for wimps."

"Goodnight, Mackenzie." She kissed me again.

"Another date. Soon."

"You can cook other dishes? Yes please. But I'll be out of town for a while. I'll call you when I return."

"Call? Ugh. Text me."

"Would you like those texts to include pictures?"

"You'd be crazy not to."

I BRUSHED my teeth and walked into the hallway. Timothy waited there, still in khakis. His dress shirt was untucked. He yawned.

"That girl is a knockout."

"As a rich jewel in an Ethiope's ear."

"It's too late for poetry."

"She's a knockout, yes, but with a great laugh."

"I asked around about Ronnie," he said. "Tonight at the gala. Everyone knows her. She attended William & Mary Law School, tough litigator, comes from money. Perhaps Roanoke's most eligible bachelorette."

"Try not to get your hopes up, old man. The stress could kill you."

"Why isn't she spending the night?"

"Virtue, maybe? At the time it seemed the right thing to do."

"I'm dubious," he said.

"All these women you sleep with, Dad? You know why they're single?"

"I'm not crazy about the phrase, 'all these women,'" he said.

"They're single because they married the wrong guy. Or chased after the wrong happiness. The woman I marry, I don't want her to be single again in ten years. And that means I do things my way. Not yours."

"You believe you'll marry her?" Timothy asked.

"Doubt it. I believe I'll marry someone. Hard to predict who."

"What do you think of Sue?"

"I like her better than Karen," I said.

"Me too. I think."

I crawled into bed a minute later. My phone chimed. A text from Ronnie. She was in bed too. Wishing me goodnight. Wearing a red nightie.

"Yowza."

16

I took a half day Monday and drove to Cave Spring High School, a blocky brick building from the 60's. The campus looked exhausted and was wisely next up on Roanoke's refurbishment list.

"Eddie drives a gold Nissan Sentra," Manny had told me. "Parks on Morning Dove Road."

I cruised the streets of Penn Forest, a large neighborhood of well-maintained houses built in the '70's and '80's. Could be Every Town America, complete with tricycles on the front lawns.

Eddie Backpack's car was exactly where Manny described, at the end of the cul-de-sac, a short walk from Cave Spring's football field. Eddie's business model impressed me. He banked on the sheer volume of student population for camouflage. Cave Spring had a thousand students, and Patrick Henry had almost two. He arrived unnoticed through the woods, blended in, surreptitiously distributed his wares through predetermined channels, and then vanished through the forested egress. Not only that, he diversified. One school in Roanoke City, and one in Roanoke County. Enterprising young man.

I waited for an hour in the baking car. We were now in

September, and temperatures had fallen five degrees from August, but I didn't notice the change. It was hot.

Eddie Backpack appeared from the forest at one, and he got into his gold Nissan, which coughed smoke from the tail. He drove north and I followed at a distance. Interstate 581 neatly cut Roanoke in half, running north to south. He drove north to Hershberger Road, as Manny had predicted, but didn't go to Valley View Mall. He turned onto Cove Road and proceeded into the Melrose Area, near Villa Heights.

Roanoke was a deeply segregated city. This part of town, had you asked white people in southern Roanoke, would be called the scary part. And by scary, they meant black. In defense of the scared white people, everyone I saw here was black. They didn't appear especially scary, though.

This part of Shenandoah Avenue consisted of long, vacant industrial parks and active salvage yards and abandoned cars. Eddie Backpack drove into a fenced gravel lot and disappeared behind a collection of derelict brick buildings that may or may not have belonged to the adjacent car parts yard. Thus far I'd escaped his notice, but tailing him inside the fenced lot didn't strike me as wise. And I'm super wise. Instead I parked on a bisecting street and waited. Across the street was an active railway yard.

Sometimes gathering intelligence is unspeakably boring. So I listened to Colin Cowherd and yelled at the radio.

Eddie was into something bigger than himself. Obviously. He wasn't manufacturing cocaine all by his lonesome. His supply had to originate somewhere, and he wouldn't be allowed to work two entire schools by himself without permission or a support system. I'd bet this collection of brick warehouses wasn't an innocent hangout.

Or perhaps he worked here, like a legitimate job. Who knew. Not me. I was just a teacher.

Sheriff Stackhouse stated that Roanoke was the halfway point between Atlanta and New York. Ergo, a good place to transfer illegal cargo. If drugs came to Roanoke and subsequently were dispersed east to Richmond, north to New York and Baltimore, west to Charles-

ton, and south to the tri-cities, then Stackhouse had a major operation under her nose with millions worth of narcotics changing hands.
Maybe billions. The FBI would get involved, because the trade
crossed state lines.

A big campaign such as that would require heavy oversight. Like
the General. And teeny-tiny itty-bitty Eddie Backpack may or may not
work for this vast network, as a simple distributor. And teeny-tiny
itty-bitty Mack August sat in his Honda, hoping to get proof.

Mack against the Machine.

That was good. I'd tell Ronnie that, for her HGTV show.

An hour later the gold Nissan emerged from the maze of brick
buildings, tires softly rolling through the old gravel. I pursued. Eddie
sped up on the street, driving far too quickly through the neighborhood off Hanover; I was forced to speed also, or else lose him. He
parked at a dilapidated house off Mercer and went inside, screen
door slamming. I wrote down the address and Eddie's license plate.
And the address for the brick warehouse complex.

Put together enough puzzle pieces and perhaps the picture would
become clear. And perhaps not.

On my way out, I passed a big black Toyota Tacoma. Driven by
Nate Silva. The Nate Silva, Master of Villainy. A kid was in the
passenger seat but I didn't get a look. Nate did a double-take at my
car. Crud. I averted my face and sped away. What awful timing. A
brutal coincidence.

Or was it?

Once past, I glanced in the rearview. Master Silva had twisted in
his seat to inspect my receding car.

Busted.

MANNY and I watched the Dodgers game that evening after Kix fell
asleep. Manny crossed his sneakers at the ankles and worked on a
scotch. Time after time, his cell phone vibrated with incoming texts.

"You're popular," I noted intelligently.

"Sí."

"Who keeps messaging?"

"Local Roanoke señoritas," Manny said.

"Ever answer?"

"Sometime. I don't know why I give them my number when they ask. Muy estúpido. Playing pool at Awful Arthurs, a girl ask. I tell her, but her friends write it down too."

"Your life is hard."

"Maybe I should use less product in my hair. Right?" he said.

"Do you tell people what you do? For a living?"

He made a gun with his finger and thumb. "Absolutely. I'm Wyatt Earp, amigo. Would you not tell people?"

"I rely on my charm and good looks."

"I use my title. You want to be Doc Holliday? I'll deputize you. Wyatt deputized Doc, in that movie. Tombstone," said Manny.

"You're Wyatt Earp?"

"Sí."

"And I'm sidekick Holliday?" I asked.

"Sí."

"You sleep on my floor."

"So?"

"I think I'm Wyatt Earp," I said.

"Was Wyatt white?"

"I don't think he was Hispanic."

"Fine, white man, you be Wyatt. You let me know, you need someone shot," said Manny.

"Maybe tomorrow night. This one's too good."

"Just you let me know. Like at the shootout corral."

I said, "You mean the OK Corral. Famous shootout between Wyatt, Virgil, Doc, and the Cowboy gang."

"Must be hard, being so smart."

"That's why I'm Wyatt, and you're not."

I stood and found my keys.

"Back in a little while."

"Going to see Ronnie," he said.

"No. Occurred to me, I haven't checked messages at my office in three weeks."

"Sure," Manny said. "Check your messages. Call it whatever you like. Check'em twice. Tell Ronnie I said hola."

I wished.

I lived five minutes from downtown. Quick drive. I parked opposite Metro, which was alive and pumping with life and vigor. And people younger than me, but probably less attractive.

The light in my office was on. How about that. Not a good sign; I didn't leave it that way. I remained in the Honda and watched the windows. Someone there? Or maybe the landlord left the light on? After three minutes, my patience was rewarded. Movement and shadow. There was a six-shot revolver in my glove compartment, and I took it out.

Not because I was scared. Rather, because I was prudent. Better safe than shot.

I took the stairs three at a time, because they creaked and snapped. A surefire warning system. If I was unable to move in stealth, at least I could move in speed. I reached the door quickly and entered, and the intruder was caught off guard.

"You," he said.

"You," I said.

It was Sergeant Sanders, the detective who resembled a Rottweiler. Beefy forearms, puffy nose. His cheeks were pink. Pistol clipped to his belt. I hadn't seen him since Stackhouse's first visit. He had the decency to look abashed.

"Find what you were looking for?"

"Ain't what it looks like, chief. I can explain," Sergeant Sanders said.

"And clean up when you're through?"

"How'd you know I was here? Got hidden cameras?"

"Preternatural instincts, only."

"Okay, okay. Put away your piece. You know how to use that thing?" Sanders asked.

"I could probably hit my foot if I tried real hard. Why are you here."

"It's your pal. The spic. New guy in the marshals office," he grunted. "He got me worried."

"The spic's name is Manny."

He shrugged.

"Right, whatever."

"What about him?"

"I looked into him. His file rang a bell. You two got the same references. You two know each other," Sanders said, with a trace of pride.

"Correct. In fact, he stays at my house."

"The hell for?"

"We're amigos," I said.

"You gay?"

"You wish."

"Yeah, well. You two being from Los Angeles, and this gang general shows up, and he's from LA. too. The one we're after."

"How do you know the General is from LA?"

"Intel. We think it's good. And the three of you guys show up within a year."

"You believe we're in cahoots, as it were," I said.

"Just making sure you wasn't."

"Weren't. Not wasn't."

"Oh, fuck off," he said, a stinging rebuke. Somehow, I regrouped.

"And what have you determined?"

"Not much." He vaguely indicated the office with his thumb. "Dunno what I'm looking for, really."

"A red jersey with Bloods stenciled on the back."

"No. I don't know. Look. I got nervous, that's all," Sanders said.

"Certainly you have no warrant."

"Come on, chief. A warrant? We're both grown-ups here."

I waffled my hand. "Eh."

"How's the teaching gig?"

"I am shockingly good at it. It wouldn't hurt your professionalism to audit the class."

"What I meant is, are you turning up leads? You're supposed to be turning up leads," he said.

"Saw a kid put gum under his desk once."

"This is important, Mack. Maybe you don't know how big."

"Do tell," I said.

"The Bloods are into prostitution. And burglary and drug pushing, and extortion. You name it. And we think it's about to get worse."

"Why do you think that?"

"I do this for a living. Damn good at it. I read the signs," Sanders said.

"Such as?"

"Such as the got'damn signs, Mack, I don't know. Call it a gut feeling."

"Ah hah," I said.

"Ah hah what?"

"We've gotten to causes of both your intrusion and your predictions. Your noble prophetic gut."

"Be serious," he said. "Gimme what you got. You got names? Suspicions? Stuff I can chase?"

"If I did, this would be neither the time nor the place."

"Why the hell not?"

"I'm tired. I caught you red-handed mere moments ago, which means I don't like you. And I'd want Stackhouse here," I said.

"The sheriff? She's a fine piece of ass, ain't she."

"I've seen worse."

"You know she's single. Gets around all over town, s'what I heard. What we all hear. Them cans ain't real," Sanders said.

"Them cans," I repeated. "Nobody says 'cans.'"

"Whatever, they're fake. Got bigger ten years ago."

"I can't believe you called them 'cans.'"

"What a pain in the ass you are."

"This I've heard," I said.

"Okay, well. Listen. You get into trouble, you call me directly. You're a jerk but you're a jerk on my side."

"So sweet, Sanders," I said. "And I didn't even buy you dinner."

17

A week passed. And nothing happened. Well, nothing except elite English classes. There were no fights at school. Ronnie was out of town. Manny shot a fugitive, directly in the left buttock, but that didn't qualify as news.

I was stymied in my attempts to locate Silva's residence. I snuck into the school's records but he only listed a post office box. Tailing him was tricky because I didn't know when he'd show up. And he knew what my car looked like.

I went back to the dojo for more mixed martial arts training. Manny came too. We jumped rope, hit bags, and sparred. He was one of those punks who rolled out of bed in peak physical form, not skinny, not fat, simply strong and long limbed. I kept up with him because I outweighed him by fifty pounds. We came home exhausted after ninety minutes.

Silva was a no-show.

Otherwise life was good. Our street smelled like fresh-cut lawn and grills, and temperatures remained in the high seventies. Kix and I played after school. He helped me spread mulch in the shade, and we watched Sesame Street on TiVo. The three adults took turns cooking dinner—steaks and salads and burgers and chicken and hotdogs.

After dinner we watched the Nationals fight the Mets for a playoff berth.

Friday night, in my bed, I was visited by an old friend.

My partner Richard, shot and deceased almost three years ago. He made periodic appearances, ushered in on the nighttime wings of doubt and worry.

What are you doing, he said, a voice full of judgement.

Trying to sleep.

Is this your life now? Are you doing it right?

I hope so. But maybe I'm just disguising and distracting the crazy inner man with a facade.

You haven't changed. Not really. You're still violent, he said. He was lying in the morgue, cold and thick like deli turkey.

Yes, but I'm healthier now.

Richard was joined by the North victims. Facedown in their own blood.

You've been off drugs and binge drinking and rampant sex and wanton fighting for a long time, they said.

Over two years.

Do you miss it?

I crave the highs. Don't miss the lows. Don't miss the depression. It's getting easier. I hope.

I rolled over, stuffed my head between the pillows.

You miss it.

Yes.

Did you fail us?

No. Maybe.

You could have prevented it.

No. I don't think so.

Teachers died at your last school. Because of you.

Life is hard. People die. I wish they didn't, but. That's what happened.

Replays of those brutal nights ran through my mind. Like a scary movie viewed too young, indelibly burnt all the way into manhood. I shook my head, jostling the memories.

We should be gone, Richard said. *But we're not. You keep dwelling on us. Manny doesn't have these demons.*

I bet he does. I'll ask him.

You're screwing everything up.

Maybe.

But I think this is simply how life works. Muddling along in the dark and hoping I'm not breaking things. Living a life of quiet desperation? More like quiet desperation and hope. And purpose.

But you're still alone.

Yes. Would being with someone change that?

Of course, Richard said.

CS Lewis said we're built with longings nothing in this life can satisfy.

What a lonely sentiment.

I bet my co-workers feel the same way. We all do. Showing up each morning with this hole inside. The worry. The doubts.

Then what is life? A vacuum?

Richard, go away.

What is life?

I read that men should be judged by their relationships.

Richard didn't say anything.

I'm doing okay with relationships.

Good relationship with Dad - check.

Good relationship with son - check.

With friends - check.

Coworkers - check, minus Ms. Deere.

Romantic life - unknown.

I hadn't heard from Ronnie recently. But I didn't need her. I liked her, but I didn't meditate on her when she was gone. Well, that wasn't true. But if I didn't see her again, I wouldn't be crushed.

The voices had abated.

My insides unclenched. The dread and worry released their grip. What a mess.

Mackenzie August, work in progress.

18

Stevie sat on my curb Saturday afternoon, kicking at rocks with the heel of his shoe. His jeans were a little too small and the T-shirt was a hand-me-down. I sat beside him, circling my knees with my arms.

"What's going on, Stevie?"

"Nothing."

"You're bored."

He kicked more pebbles into the street.

"Yeah. I got nothing to do."

"Your foster brother around?" I asked.

"Naw. He's always gone, mostly."

"Must be," I said. "I don't even know what he looks like."

"He friends with these older kids. He don't always wanna, but they come get him. Get him into trouble."

"What kind of trouble?" I asked.

"Bad grades. Fights. Bad stuff. I think he's in a gang."

"That sucks."

"Yeah."

"What kind of gang?" I asked.

"Dunno. Stuff with drugs."

"You can always come hang out here, at my house. Right? You know that?"

"Yeah, thanks, Mr. August."

"My house is kinda boring too, though, huh."

"Nah, but mine's got an Xbox."

We talked a few more minutes, until an unmarked police car turned the corner. Stevie identified it immediately.

"Oh crud," he said.

"It's okay. Not here for you," I said.

"Sometimes is. For my mom. Or Mr. Earl. Cops come, you know, and stuff gets weird."

"Not today."

"Still. I'm going back to Mr. Earl's. Bye." Stevie got up and ran quickly down the sidewalk.

Ah, youthful knees. I stood up, a slower process than in bygone days.

My neighbor's sprinkler was running. That twit. His lawn radiated verdancy already, making mine more of a grayish green by comparison. Maybe I'd cut his hose.

The police car stopped in front of me. Window buzzed down and Sheriff Stackhouse said, "Get in, if you got a minute."

"Park around back," I said. "Have a margarita."

"Best idea of the day." She pulled into the driveway and stepped out. Took off her aviators and nestled them into her hair. She pressed her hands into the small of her back, stretched backwards and produced a grunting noise, and then retrieved a folder from her car. She followed me inside and I poured her a glass from the pitcher. "Homemade," she said.

"Only the best."

"I like a man knows his way around the kitchen." Her voice wasn't deep but it was husky. Used to issuing orders and shouting. She drained half the glass. "Jeez, you're a big guy, Mack. You use steroids?"

"Used to. College and California. Not in three or four years."

"Personal question, sorry."

"No sweat. Someone told me, and I quote, that your cans aren't real. True?"

She laughed, a delighted throaty sound I worried would wake Kix from his nap. "Turnabout is fair play. Hell no they aren't real. Are you kidding? Look at me."

"If you insist."

"Sad to say, Mackenzie, but they were the best decision I ever made. That and Botox. I went from insecure to a hard-ass. Detective to sheriff."

"Wow. Those are some magic boobs."

"I'll say. Men are such predictable mouth-breathers, they work wonders. Do you know, you're the first person to directly ask me in five years? Everyone else gossips behind my back."

"Do they ruin your credibility? As an officer of the law?"

"Often, to the weak-minded. And whether I should or not, I feel the need to prove myself. Kinsey Millhone said it best, that I need to show I'm as tough as the guys, which I'm happy to report isn't that difficult. And I look hot as hell doing it. But, enough about my tits, perhaps?"

"Sure."

"Look at these," she said. She pushed the folder into my hands and I opened it. Glossy photos of a dead body. "Anna Beth Collins. Recently found dead. Junior at Botetourt High School. Her friends say she liked to party and she came to Roanoke to see some guy. They don't know who. Cocaine residue in her nostrils."

"Gang markings on the ankle."

She nodded. "Bloods. Anna Beth is pretty, so this one will be all over the news."

"I've been at the center of that storm. It's no fun."

"This new Bloods general is a vicious bastard," she said.

"Something doesn't ring true, though."

"Talk to me, Mackenzie. You're this big city homicide detective. Stories about you are legendary, enough to make me swoon. What have you learned? What do you know? Why doesn't it ring true?"

"This pattern of murdering high school girls. Even for gang rites of passage, it's unusually violent. Violent and unwise, because they're calling unnecessary attention to themselves."

"So?"

"If the gangs were truly as violent and uncontrolled as these murders indicate, the brutality would spill over into other areas. There'd be more rumbles in the slums. More fights at the mall. Shootings. Burglaries. But there aren't. All other areas of the enterprise appear to be orderly, for lack of a better word."

"You know how it is. The gangbangers aren't particularly intelligent. They choose a dangerous path, armed with the foreknowledge it will lead to jail or the grave. But they do it anyway. Like animals. Murdering these girls doesn't strike me as out of character," she said.

"They aren't well educated, I agree, but that doesn't imply a lack of intelligence. They are street smart, and they survive a brutal lifestyle. In most areas, Roanoke's gangs appear to exercise restraint, but not the rites of passage."

She finished her margarita, cleaned the corners of her mouth with her thumb and forefinger, and pulled them together at her lower lip. "Okay. Why?" she asked.

"No idea. I thought you were the sheriff."

"Not a very good one, apparently."

"Just a great pair of cans?" I asked.

"Hah. No one says cans, Mackenzie, after the sixth grade."

"No one says gangbangers anymore either."

"Tell me about the school. Those students know everything. What have you heard?" she asked.

"I have a few leads but I'm not ready to share yet."

The photo of Anna Beth Collins was laying on the counter, and she tapped it with her finger. "This isn't a research project. People are getting hurt."

"If I tell you what I know, you'll chase and scare the leads. I'm working on it," I said.

"You need to tell me, soon as you can. Our Gang and Narcotics guys are getting nothing. Which corroborates your theory that these sets are well disciplined," she said.

"He could be a ghost. This General? Maybe he's only a rumor."

"Maybe. But he has a title. Everyone I've interrogated refers to him as the General. That's unusual for a gang. Makes me think it's a real person."

Timothy August parked beside Sheriff Stackhouse's car. We heard the crunch of tires. He came inside with two bags of groceries purchased from the farmers' market. He wore the blue shorts with little whales on them, topsiders, and a linen shirt.

"Sheriff Stackhouse. What an honor. You'll stay for dinner?"

"Timothy, you're looking well. Dinner? With you? I wish, but that's three hours away. No, I've got places to be, but I appreciate the gesture. How is your elementary school? Crystal Spring, right?"

"We're humming along nicely. Holy hell, that's quite a photograph on the counter. Not all of us are accustomed to brutality."

Stackhouse collected her folder and files, took a grape from one of Dad's bags, and made eye contact with me. "Keep in touch, Mackenzie." Then she was gone.

19

I took another half day Monday, recruited Manny for an afternoon operation, and waited at the cul-de-sac in Penn Forest near Cave Spring High School. And near the gold Nissan. Like clockwork, Eddie Backpack appeared around two. I was unwilling to bust my cover, as the kids say, so I ducked down in my seat, windows cracked, and peeked over the top, and listened, the same way Superman would do.

Eddie Backpack was wearing Nikes and baggy jeans and a red T-shirt. He froze when he saw Manny leaning against his car. Manny had a pistol and badge clipped to his belt, and a marshal's cap on. He tipped the cap backwards, like he was in a Western.

"Afternoon, Eddie."

Eddie didn't say anything.

"Got a couple questions for you, hombre."

Eddie took off like a sprinter. He was a young guy, maybe eighteen, and moving on legs like whips. He bolted past a house and plowed into the shrubs. Manny took the easier route on the far side of the house. I jogged along behind, rounding the residence in time to see Eddie trip on an exposed maple tree root. He got up in time for

Manny to hit him like a linebacker. Leading with his shoulder and sending Eddie sprawling onto Barn Swallow Road.

I'm glad Manny was on my side.

Eddie tried to get up, but Manny put a hard right into his ribs and then an elbow to the back of his head.

"Try this again," Manny said. "Afternoon, Eddie. Got a couple questions for you."

"Police brutality," Eddie choked.

"No, señor, we haven't gotten to the brutal part. 'Sides, I'm chasing a felon resisting arrest."

Blood was flowing from Eddie's chin from his impact with the street.

"Felon? Bitch, I ain't no felon."

This cute little street with cute suburbia homes was no place for an interrogation. Manny hauled him up by the backpack and forced him into the side yard under a shady oak with long branches. I stayed behind an olive green house, the kind with a garage hidden within its structure so it looks bigger than reality.

"Simply wanna talk, Eddie. Why you running? Something to hide?"

"No, man. That hurt, man, what the hell."

"This goes the right way, amigo, you get to walk away. We ain't here for you," Manny said. His hands were on his hips. He wasn't a gigantic man but he towered over cowering Eddie Backpack.

"We?"

"Me. You don't hear so good."

Eddie was a pale-skinned guy with a small afro, the kind which holds a hair pick well. He has a wispy goatee, still only a kid.

"The fuck you want?"

"I know you're moving dice in Patrick Henry and Cave Spring. I want to know who you work for," Manny said. "You tell me, you go free, hombre. Never bother you again."

"Don't know nothing about dice."

"Lemme see that backpack."

"Got a warrant?"

Manny hit him in the nose. A soft pop, just enough to hurt, make his eyes water. Eddie cursed and staggered a step. "Warrant? No warrant. No need," Manny said. He hit him again, another bop to the nose. Now it began to bleed.

Come on, Manny. Better ways to do this.

Intrepid and stalwart men such as myself should not be hiding behind houses. I felt like a coward.

"Jesus, man, what the hell," whined Eddie.

"I know that backpack was stuffed with coke earlier. Now it's full of cash. Am I right?"

Eddie didn't answer. Just cradled his nose.

"Soon you're going to head north." Manny pulled out a slip of paper and read off the address of the industrial warehouse park I'd seen Eddie drive into. Eddie knew the address and he groaned. "What's there, Eddie? What's in those warehouses?"

"Don't know nothing," he muttered.

"After that, you go home? Go home to Mama?" Manny read off the other address, this one of the home I'd seen him go into.

"What do you want, man?"

"Already told you. You're a Blood, working for a local set. You push cocaine at the schools, but I'm giving you the chance of a life-time. I'm letting you go free, Eddie. Because I'm not after you."

Eddie scowled and didn't talk.

"Answer a few questions. Go back to your Nissan. Never mention this. How's that sound, amigo? Sí?"

"What? What do you want?"

"Who lives in that house? At the address?"

"I live at home. With Ma. And my sister," Eddie said.

"Keep going."

"I pay the bills. Mama's got glaucoma and blood pressure."

"You keep twenty percent of what you make?"

"Closer to twenty-five." He said it with a trace of pride. I didn't blame him. Within the world in which he grew up, he was running good. Successful. Couldn't judge kids like this by my standards, growing up with a mom and dad and money.

"What's the name of your set? Are you in the Rollin' Kennedys?"

"Yeah. Rollin' Kennedys."

"Talk about the warehouse," Manny said.

"It's a warehouse."

"Go on."

"Trucks come in, stop at the warehouse, and we unload certain boxes. Then the trucks move on, to Walmart and shit. You know?"

"Who runs the warehouse?"

"Man, listen. I'm dead this gets out."

For a moment, Manny displayed a note of humanity. He put his hand on Eddie's shoulder and leaned down to look him in the eye. "Sorry about hitting you, amigo. Had to get your attention. Truly, I'm not after you. Bigger fish. Okay? Get it? Your name never gets mentioned. You come out of this alive. Who runs the warehouse?"

"Big Will."

"Big Will."

"Yeah. Little guy, stocky, busted nose, Big Will," Eddie said. "Busted nose like me. Damn."

"How high up does Big Will go?"

Eddie shrugged. "He's got a couple guys like me who deliver. Guy who guards the stash. That kinda shit."

"Big Will is a Rollin' Kennedy."

"Yeah."

"He a leader in the set? A general?" Manny asked.

"General? Nah, man."

"Tell me about Nate Silva."

"Master Nate?" Eddie looked surprised. "Master Nate a freelancer. He's everywhere, kinda."

"He's in your set?"

"Maybe. He says he is. But he also say he's a Lincoln."

"Does Big Will answer to Master Nate?" Manny asked.

"Maybe. I don't ask a lot of questions, man."

Manny kept his hand on Eddie's shoulder but looked up at me and my hiding spot. I pulled out my phone and texted him. Manny looked at the texts, nodded, and said, "These girls keep dying, Eddie. In the news."

"I know. Messed up."

"Why are the Bloods getting violent?"

Eddie shook his head. He still held his nose, giving him nasal tones. "Don't know. Don't nobody know."

"It's gotta stop."

"Don't look at me."

"Tell me about the General," Manny said.

Eddie laughed.

Manny asked, "What's funny?"

"Nobody knows the General. Maybe Big Will does. Maybe not."

"You think he exists?"

"Yeah. People scared of him. Meet him in the dark. Crazy motherfucker."

That was enough.

I turned and went up the hill, past the house. Got in the car and drove to a side street. Four minutes later, Eddie rolled past in the Nissan and I went to fetch Manny.

He ducked into the passenger seat and said, "Hola, Master August. Learn anything?"

"You throw a mean elbow."

"You like hiding behind houses?"

"No," I said. "That was the worst."

"Sissy."

20

Kix and I loaded the stroller with juice, snacks, toys, and the diaper bag. So armed, we could survive Armageddon. He sat alertly in the chair, leaning forward into the restraint and barking out unintelligible orders.

We strolled downtown and pursued the Party at Elmwood. Some band I'd never heard of occupied the stage and the crowd of five thousand urbanites, which spilled out and up the amphitheater. Venders erected booths along the walks, and angular long-limbed youths threw frisbees and their dogs barked, and Kix glared at morons chasing imaginary digital stuff on their phones. I wore flip-flips with my jeans and polo shirt.

I bought a Deschutes beer and a gyro from a food truck and we stopped to rest on a big rock at the top of the park, near Jefferson.

"Mr. August! We see you everywhere, man."

It was Jeriah again, the loud-mouthed running back in my first period class. He was with his father, a tall man drinking beer from a plastic cup. He wore black alligator loafers, black cotton slacks, and a black belt with gold buckle. Tight gray T-shirt. Powerful guy, his muscles were high and tight. We shook hands.

"Mr. August," he greeted.

"Call me Mackenzie," I said, "and I'll call you Marcus."

"Got a deal."

Jeriah was with a few buddies I didn't recognize and they wandered away.

"I saw you at church last Sunday," Marcus said.

"Oh yeah? You attend St. Johns?"

"Yes, last few years." He took a drink from the cup. "My wife's in the choir."

"I don't know much about churches or denominations," I said. "I picked it because of the interesting architecture."

"Hell, I don't think denominations matter much. Ask me, the Almighty gets a little tired of our demarcations."

"I was God, I'd get tired of pretty much everything we do," I said.

"Look at my son." He nodded down the sidewalk, toward the library. "Look how important this clique is to them. Look how they swell with pride. Do you know why?"

"Inclusion."

"I agree, Mackenzie, but it's more than that. Once your boy gets older, you'll see. The best part of being included is keeping others out. Otherwise, what's the damn point?"

He spoke with a deep voice, rich with feeling and thought.

"Inclusion isn't enough?"

"Should be. Probably is, for some. But for the insecure, excluding others is too sweet."

"They're all insecure," I said. "We're doomed."

"Same with my church. We're Episcopal and we look down on the Anglicans. They're too rigid. We look down on the Methodists. Look down on the heathens. On the Muslims. The foreigners. On everyone."

"How about on black people?"

"No no. Far too sophisticated for that. But just so happens, we're one of only two black families there. So something doesn't match up." He shook his head, frustrated and angry like this was a subject always boiling under the surface. "Look. Just look at those boys. With their best friends and they keep staring at their damn phones. Life passes them by and they gape at screens. A big reason? Insecurity and exclusion. Sometimes they call each other and don't say a thing. Not a damn thing, just have the phone to their ear. Look at me, I'm important. More important than you."

"We adults do it too," I said. "What good is going to a cocktail party if the planet doesn't know you went?"

"Exactly." He pointed his finger at me in approval. I'm the best. "Precisely. The curse of Facebook. Of social media. Look at me, look at what I do. Exclusion. How are we going to raise young men of integrity? Young men of determination and grit, when all is surface and flash? I tell you, Mackenzie, I just don't know."

"You're getting me fired up. I may enroll Kix in the Army tomorrow."

"Know what I was doing when I was Jeriah's age? Hustling. I delivered papers in Miami in high school. Raised my little brother by myself. Delivered papers before school and worked at a department store after. Stole cologne test bottles and sold them for extra scratch. You understand? Not proud of it, but I hustled. Jeriah, now, doesn't like getting out of bed. After school he goes to practice, and then doesn't want to do his homework. I give him the world on a plate and he makes worse grades than I did."

"We learn obedience through suffering," I said.

"You're quoting Hebrews. The son of man learned through suffering." He shook his head and sniffed, arms crossed over his chest, cup empty. "My son doesn't suffer enough. Same with our church. Zero suffering, so we focus our energies on keeping people out. Politics. Same with my business. Bickering over territory and rights."

"What do you do?" I asked.

"Real estate. Development. Investing. Enough to go around, more than enough work, but pride gets in the way. End up hurting one another instead of focusing on the big picture."

The sun had dipped behind the western skyline and temperatures were dropping.

"You're an intense guy, Marcus," I said.

"Like I said, it's hard work raising boys. I think on it, quite a bit.

Never let minor details get in the way of the big picture. The big picture is we do our best, work hard, and advance the community in which we live. Sorry for preaching at you, Mackenzie, but you appear a kindred spirit. A man who looks like he'll break a few rules to get after what he needs. I like that in an educator. Our boys don't need syllabuses, they need men to follow."

"The strength and power of a country depend absolutely on it."

"You're quoting again, but I don't know it." He stuck out his hand again, and we shook. "I need to round the herd. We'll have you over for dinner soon. We'll talk faith and religion and boys and society and all of its flaws."

"And maybe some of its redemption."

"Hell yes. Give me your number."

I did. He said goodbye and turned to find the teenagers, who'd flocked to a group of young women.

I looked at Kix. "You catch all that?"

He shrugged.

21

After school on Thursday, I hustled to the warehouses off Shenandoah, near the train tracks. Big Will interested me. I wanted to see the man in the flesh. Manny researched him in the government database and came up with a photo. So I had a face.

I settled behind the wheel, a block removed from the entrance, and listened to ESPN radio.

Coffee. I forgot coffee. Never stakeout without coffee.

At four, Ronnie texted me. My heart leaped and hope sprang eternal.

>> **I'm in Roanoke again**

>> **I miss you. And your house.**

>> **And Kix.**

>> **If you'll still have me...**

>> **...I would like to eat your cooking again.**

She included a selfie. She was at work, sitting at a desk. Hair up in a ponytail, makeup a little heavier than usual, green jewel-toned blouse. She looked tired. Her smile, while still a ten out of ten, lacked some heat. Like she'd lost some mischievous energy.

Salmon? Mexican? Italian? Burgers?

Steak? Salad? Seafood?

>> **Surprise me.**

>> **=)**

>> **At your earliest convenience.**

BIG WILL EMERGED AT FIVE.

Big Will was big, if not tall. And fierce. Not at all like the happy squat gentleman I'd pictured, based incorrectly off Eddie Backpack's tone and description. He didn't look like his photo either. His Dickies were tight, his stride purposeful. The red hoodie bulged at the biceps. He was maybe thirty-five, a grizzly beard and shaved head. Tattoos up his neck. Nose flat and misshapen. He pointed and barked and the men with him nodded and left to do his bidding. In a hurry.

He got into a big truck, similar to Nate Silva's, but he didn't drive far. He stopped at someplace called the Addisonian Social Club, which crawled with activity. I parked a block away and watched. Big Will was popular, greeted as soon as he closed the truck's door. Women in jeans with curves for days and gold belts came to get hugs. The Addisonian looked fun, but appeared to cater mostly to black folks.

I didn't know whether to call them black, African-American, or people of color. I wanted to use the appropriate term, but I didn't know which it was. Whatever. I would stick out at the Addisonian, and I didn't want to stick out.

He went inside with a group of partiers. Music and light throbbed out until the door closed again. Now that's a party.

Should I go in? Or should I go get Kix and some tacos?

I flipped a coin.

Kix it is. The coin didn't matter. He always wins.

22

My son had a nightmare at two in the morning. Or if not a nightmare, whatever it is that wakes toddlers up with a start in the middle of the night.

Manny leapt to his feet, magnum in his fist.

He was clammy with sweat and the pistol trembled and gleamed. He stared at me and I watched awareness reboot like a computer behind his eyes. Until then, I made no sudden movements. Better safe than shot.

"Sorry," he said.

He dropped the weapon onto his pillow and left the room. I followed. Kix stood in his crib, eyes wet with tears. Manny lifted him and sat in the rocking chair.

"I got him, Mack. Back to bed with you."

Kix seemed puzzled but pacified by this arrangement.

Instead, I laid down on the rug in Kix's room and rubbed at my eye sockets with the heels of my hands. The room was small and smelled like diapers and baby powder. Streetlights threw in rays between the blinds, and the air swirled with dust. The house had that sacred quiet only achieved at two in the morning.

"You having a nightmare too, Manny?"

"Nah. Just, like, this tension I can't let go. Constant stress."

"Do dead bodies ever talk to you? At night?" I asked, thinking about Richard and the North victims.

"At night. And during the day."

"What do they say?"

"Say? Nada. They scream." He chuckled, like a soft snort through his nose. Kix was already fading back to sleep.

I grabbed a stuffed monkey and used it as a pillow. "Why does this happen? I hear dead people too."

"I dunno, amigo. Guilt? Trauma? That's above my pay grade."

"Mine too," I yawned.

"You got faith, right? You should know. Look it up in the Bible."

"I don't think it works that way."

"If you don't know, I got no chance," Manny said.

"I'll ask God. See what he says. But it'll probably be a secret."

"Secret? From me? What, God's a racist?"

"No, he just doesn't like you. Told me so himself," I said.

"He does too. I hope so. I really need the next life to be better than this one."

From my vantage I could see under Kix's crib—pacifiers and stuffed animals. I said, "This one is growing on me."

"We got damaged souls, big Mack. We won't get in to the party upstairs."

"Damaged yet beautiful," I said. "We got a chance. We'll rely on grace."

"That's why we hear the corpses, you know, amigito. Broken souls are the natural consequences of shooting people in the ass. We're paying the price."

"We talk about some deep stuff in the middle of the night, Manuel."

"Wanna smoke?" He yawned so big his jaw cracked. "I got weed."

"I'm two years clean. I'm good. Kix's asleep, so you go ahead." I stood up and took my son and placed him back in the crib.

"Not unless you do."

"I'm going back to bed," I said.

"Me too."

"The guest bed might be more comfortable, you know."

"Nah," he said. We shuffled back into my room. "There is no sleep without you."

"You're broken. You should have shot fewer people in the ass."

"I haven't even started yet."

23

After first period, between classes as the hall was throttled with hormones, I stood by Reginald Willis. He wore a sweater, as he did every day no matter the heat.

"Mr. August, you need a good shave, sir. How then shall the children learn? You, looking like a bum," he said.

"Willis, you ever heard about the Addisonian Social Club?"

He turned to regard me from the corner of his eye. His mouth cracked a smile but for once was silent. For several seconds.

"What'cho want with the Addisonian?"

"A friend mentioned it."

"A friend." He cackled, a burst of sound that startled the passersby. "A friend. You're a lying white man."

"What? I have friends."

"The Addisonian." He shook his head.

"Enlighten me."

"It's a club. Dancing. You know?"

"You ever go?" I asked.

"Of course. Old Reggie got moves, youngster."

"Can I go?"

Another long pause. His expression was full of mirth and suspicion. "Why?"

"Because."

"Who you going with?" he asked.

"Does it matter?"

He nodded. "It does."

"I'll go with you."

"The hell you will! Old Reginald showing up with this funny-looking white man. My women would eat you alive, Mr. August, and enjoy every minute. They're like jackals."

"It's a club exclusively for people of color?"

"People of color," he said. His tone was mocking. "Call me black, Mr. August, 'cause I call you white. People who fret over such distinctions got nothing better to do. Hurry up, children! The bell tolls for thee! And no sir, the Addisonian is not exclusive to brothers and sisters."

"But."

"But. You'd be the only one, most times."

"Maybe—"

"The Addisonian is a place where I go to cut loose. All are welcome, Mr. August, but white people don't have fun. Don't know how. Too uptight. You understand? You can go, sure, but you'd be like Trump at a black church. You don't look a man who can get down."

"It's a good time?"

"The Addisonian? Best place in Roanoke. Good for my soul."

"You know a guy, Big Will?"

His face clouded and all laughter drained away. He grabbed me by the elbow. "Listen here, Mr. August, you come talk to me after school. You understand? And don't say that name again."

The bell rang. He gave me an extra hard squeeze and released.

CLASSES ENDED. The school drained of students and noise, like a balloon deflating. Sudden silence.

I glanced in Ms. Bennett's room. Her room was tossed and shaken, desks and papers everywhere. She sat in a student's desk, legs splayed, a far-off look. A spitball was lodged in her hair.

"I don't even know what happened," she said to herself.

She was drowning in the deep end. I'd offered ranks of suggestions but she still wasn't brave enough to pull the proverbial trigger. She'd start swimming soon or sink to the bottom, and nothing I could do to change it.

I moseyed into Reginald Willis's room. He sat at his desk and overwhelmed the chair. He glowered.

"So it's true."

"The rumors about how much I bench? I hope so," I said.

"You think this is a joke, boy."

"That's just how I interpret the world, Reginald. I joke. What's true?" I asked.

"You're a cop."

"'Fraid not."

"Bull," he said.

"Cross my heart."

"Don't matter. The rumors say you are, so that's the truth. The students find out, you're busted."

"I'm not a police officer. I used to be."

"Why are you asking about Big Will?" Reginald asked.

"You know him?"

"Everyone knows him! So, what? You part of the war on drugs? You gentrifying your students? Come to save us with your whiteness?"

I grabbed a chair from the wall and set it down across his desk. Sat in it. "Mr. Willis, I've upset you. I'm sorry. Can you explain? I've taken away all your joy and I don't know why."

He leaned back in his chair and his thick fingers drummed on the desk. He made a low grunting noise. "You used to be a cop?"

"In Los Angeles. Quit two years ago. You dislike cops?"

"I do. Well, that ain't right. I think they often cause more trouble than needs be. More trouble than they solve. Only cops allowed in the hood should be from the hood. You get it?"

"I do."

"Why you asking about Big Will?" Reginald asked.

"I'm not sure I trust you. Like you said, if the students get the wrong idea, if you start talking, I'm busted."

"Mr. August, I'm a teacher. Coulda been a preacher. Right? Got me a degree in paralegal studies from Richmond, could be working for a judge. But I teach. You understand that? I grew up off Melrose, and went to college 'cause of the grace of God and my eleventh grade math teacher, Mr. Fowler. My daughter, she's a nurse. My other daughter, she's married an accountant and I got two grandkids. Happily married these twenty-seven years. I'm mad at'cha, Mr. August, because you're in trouble. Or about to be. So maybe you tell me why you asking about Big Will."

"Students in my class are buying and selling cocaine. I found the notes and I found the delivery system. I don't want to ruin their lives so I haven't reported. Instead I've done research and discovered Big Will."

"You discovered Big Will," he repeated.

"Right."

"And you haven't told about the coke."

"Ms. Deere has no idea," I said. "Nor do the other administrators."

"Well then. Not as dumb as you look. Maybe hope for you."

"Why's that?"

"You think jail cures problems? You think kids go to Coyner Springs and come out good people? Naw. Drugs ain't the problem. Drugs are a coping mechanism. Drugs are a currency, a market, a pain reliever. And also drugs are the devil. But the police don't offer any solutions. Jail acts like a school for criminals, you understand."

"You and I are on the same page," I said.

"No we ain't, neither. What good you think you'll do with Big Will? You think he's the only way kids get drugs? You take him out and your problems are solved?"

"Tell me about him."

"He came through these halls. Twenty years ago, maybe. I was here. I remember Big Will. Enterprising young man. Good student. He'll kill you, Mr. August. He will. Won't even stop eating lunch to do it."

"You're scared of him."

"I respect him. Same way I respect violence. See, Mr. August, the drugs are everywhere. You think you'll stop them? Try stopping cancer instead. Got a better chance. Big Will's got a big operation and you won't stop it. You do? And someone else will pick it up. Can't stop time. And you can't stop this."

"Your solution is to be a role model?"

"Same solution as Mr. Fowlers, my math teacher. Teach the truth. Be a role model. Kids who come from money will go on to have money. Kids who don't, won't. What's gonna change that cycle? Nothing. 'Cept maybe me. Not the police. Not the drugs. But you pick the hill you want to die on, Mr. August, and some hills can't be conquered."

"Where'd you hear I was a cop?"

He shrugged and waved the question away. "People talk. Teachers gossip. You stay away from Big Will."

"I'm not sure I can do that."

"Well. Then. S'been nice knowing you, Mr. August."

24

My cellphone rang at eight. The days were getting shorter, and eight was dark now. Kix and I were rocking and reading *Goodnight Moon* for the nine hundredth time. I answered the phone.

"Speak to Mackenzie August, please," the voice said.

"This is your lucky day."

"Mr. August, this is Adam Moseley. I'm a local attorney and I function as guardian ad litem for Steven Wells. Does the name ring a bell?"

"Little Stevie down the street, sure." I had the phone pinned between my cheek and shoulder, and Kix was babbling at the book.

"I'm here at the Rescue Mission and so is Steven. He needs a ride home, which I'm happy to provide, but I wondered if you'd mind coming down for a chat. I know this is late," he said.

"I don't mind. How can I help? What's he doing there?"

"He ends up here every few months, looking for his mom. It's complicated. He's mentioned you a few times."

"Be there in twenty minutes."

"Thanks. I'm in the women and children's shelter."

I put Kix into the crib with a handful of books and toys, and I changed out of my sweats into jeans and sneakers. Dad was in his room, still wearing work clothes, lying atop his made bed and watching documentaries on Netflix.

"You always make your bed, huh."

"We don't make our bed, we're no better than savages," he said. "That's what separates us."

"Gotta run out for a few. Keep an ear out for Kix?"

"Certainly. You're going to see Ronnie?"

"I wish."

The Rescue Mission was an impressive homeless shelter, in effect, which took up several city blocks off Elm. Cafeteria, classrooms, secondhand store, temporary apartments, bunk rooms, showers — it was quite the operation. I parked in front of the women's shelter and went in.

The first person I saw was Ronnie. She sat in a rocking chair inside a play area, and she was surrounded by a silent audience of young children. She held a picture book open on her lap and turned pages as she read. *Cyrus and the Unsinkable Serpent*, by Bill Peet. I read it when I was little. This was the goodnight story for the kids at the shelter.

My heart, the scoundrel, betrayed me and leapt into my throat.

Between pages, Ronnie glanced up to smile at the audience. Her eyes found mine, widened in surprise, and locked on. Our colliding gazes created such heat I'm surprised the kids didn't notice. I began to melt.

Stevie was standing with Adam Moseley. I'd met Adam once in a courtroom last year, though he didn't remember. Former Navy JAG, now he owned his own law firm. Thick through the shoulders, strong hands, knuckles like battleships. He was still dressed for a courtroom, sports coat hanging limp in his hand.

"Mr. August, thanks for coming in. Steven says you're aware of his situation."

"Some of it."

He led us to a conference room behind the front desk and the three of us sat. Stevie sat on his hands and stared at his sneakers.

"You're a big guy. Should play rugby for the local team," Moseley said.

"No thanks, I like my face."

"Here's the deal. I've been involved with Steven and his family for three years. I represented his dad but he got ten years anyway."

"So, you suck."

"More than you know, but in this case ten years was sheer mercy. Could have been thirty." He was tired and rubbed his eyes. He had a good voice for bawling orders on a Navy ship, deep and authoritative. "I've worked to reunite Steven with his mother but she's failed four drug tests. Steven is a great kid, deserves a lot better than this, so I'm not giving up."

"I made the honor roll last year," Stevie said.

"Atta boy. How can I help?"

"Well, you can't. Not really. Certainly not officially. But off the books, I'd like as many eyes as I can get on Steven. He's convinced his mom will show up at the Rescue Mission any day, so he runs the two miles or whatever and gets stuck."

"Is he allowed to see his mom?" I asked.

"Supervised visits. So not really."

"He's welcome at my place any time he wants. Have you met Earl, the foster father?" I asked.

"I have. Good guy, for the most part. Strict disciplinarian, which I like."

"Drinks too much," I said.

"They all do. Every damn one of them. But Steven's got a better situation than most. Which means he's fed, clothed, and stable."

Stevie said, "And he's got an Xbox."

"If you could ask how he's doing. Ask about his grades. Ask about school and stuff like that, it'd help Steven out a lot," Moseley said. "We need eyes, ears, and attention on this young man. Ever see signs of mistreatment, I need to know. Ask to see his report card. He looks hungry, feed him. And, he starts thinking about making a dash for the Rescue Mission? You call me first."

"Yeah, sure. Happy to. Keep my number handy, if you think of other stuff. Does Earl drive?"

"Yes, but this late he's already two beers in," Moseley said.

"I'll drive Stevie home. He lives a couple houses down."

"Great." He stood and glanced at his watch. "I hurry home, I get to listen to my eldest read *Harry Potter* to the younger two."

We shook hands and he left.

The play area was empty. Kids gone to bed. No sign of Ronnie.

Argh. Better to have loved and lost, I suppose.

My pulse would relax any minute. Hopefully.

Stevie got into the passenger seat and I drove him up Elm toward Grandin.

"Think your mom's gonna show up at the Rescue Mission, huh?" I said.

"Hope so. Ain't seen her since before summer."

"You're a good guy, Stevie. All these struggles are going to make you into a strong man, and you're going to help a lot of people one day. Right?" I said.

"Maybe."

"What's going on with your foster brother?"

"He's joining a gang. Gets beat up and stuff a lot," Stevie said. Said it matter-of-factly, like the sky is blue.

"Where are his parents? Do you know?"

"No, never ever talks about them."

I asked, "Want to spend the night with us? Same spare bedroom as last time."

"No thanks, Mr. August, I like my bed."

I pulled in front of Earl's house, a two-story craftsman in need of some TLC. Wild honeysuckle vines choked the gutters, and shutters hung loose. If he spent twenty thousand on restorations it'd be worth a quarter million, which is big money in Roanoke where the living is cheap. Earl sat on the front porch steps. Night had fallen but the house was dark, a single light on upstairs. Stevie got out, and Earl gave me a halfhearted wave.

I watched until Stevie went inside. Couldn't solve everyone's problems, I supposed. Sure wished I could. I'd be a role model and teach the truth, like Reginald Willis and Mr. Fowler. Some days, it didn't seem enough. I drove on.

A red Mercedes was in my driveway. The girl leaning against it lit up the yard. Ronnie was dressed in crimson booties, skinny jeans, and a diaphanous spaghetti strap blouse. Her arms were crossed.

"My apartment is big," she said. "And empty. And cold. Sometimes I hate going home."

My throat threatened to constrict and my chest turned icy. Battle stations, all hands.

"Want a drink?"

"You don't need to entertain me, Mackenzie. I shouldn't have come here. I'm lonely, is all. I just want to look at you. All I need is to be in a house with people who love each other, even if I don't belong. I want to smell your couch and your cologne, and... And I don't know. Just for a few minutes?"

I opened the door for her and held out my hand. "You belong. Come in and smell my couch."

She laughed, that rosiest of all notes, but her eyes had spilled over. She took my hand in hers and kissed it. I led her to the kitchen. She sat at the wooden table and took shaky breaths.

"I'm sorry, Mackenzie. It's been...it's been a long day. A long week."

"All I have is beer. That okay?"

"Yes. Please."

I fetched two Oktoberfests, and sat next to her. Put my hand on hers. She flinched but didn't retract, and she took a long drink.

"Stuff you can talk about?" I asked.

"No. Not really. I'm not even sad, really, more like frustrated. Mad."

"Family trauma?" I asked.

She nodded.

"Yes, for the most part. Like I told you previously, I'm full of awful secrets and sin."

"Three of them."

She nodded and finished the beer. Wow.

I asked, "Want another?"

"No. You're kind."

"Damsel in distress, you know. Can't resist," I said.

"I'm an attorney, buster. I'm not a damsel. And I'm never in distress." She cocked her chin upwards.

"It's reverse sexism to pretend girls are never girls and never experience distress. That creates faulty and impossible standards, like magazine covers."

"I know. I was kidding." She emitted a short effeminate burp. "Feminism only carries one so far, I've found, in my scant years practicing. I think at the end of the day, we suffer from the same human conditions everyone else does."

"Money can't buy happiness, it turns out?"

"At least not yet. I'm all kinds of distressed."

"I know the feeling," I said.

"You do?"

"Of course. I get nightmares in the form of dead bodies."

"Doesn't seem like you can be distressed. You're like, maybe, a mountain. Come what may, you won't be moved. No, wait! I can do better. This house is the mountain, and everyone in here is safe. And you take the safety with you when you leave."

"Wow, and all you had is one beer."

"It's not the beer. I'm trying to explain the mysterious. You know what it is? About you? It's that you know who you are. And so does this house. It's grounded. And I feel better here."

"You're a mess."

"But a cute one?" she asked.

"Like the sunshine. Why were you at the Rescue Mission?"

"I volunteer a couple evenings a week. My father says it's white guilt," Ronnie said.

"You're a lawyer. A bartender. And you volunteer at homeless shelters. I'm starstruck."

"I'm flexible, too," she said.

"Prove it."

She grinned.

"The last time we were together?" she said. "I thought about you for a week. Did you think about me?"

"I did."

"This can't get serious, Mackenzie. We're two lonely people. Okay? That's all."

"Ronnie, I'll be honest. I'm not lonely. Not really. I like you. It's that simple. Anything else would be sweeping emotions under the rug, or pretending I'm happy to see you just because I'm lonely. But fact is, I'm not. If it was loneliness, any girl would do."

"You like me just because you like me?"

"Yes."

"Oh gosh." She lowered her head to the table. "What are you doing?"

"What do you mean?"

"Are you trying to get my clothes off? Just ask. It's easy."

I squeezed her hand. "That's not why I said it."

"That doesn't make sense, Mackenzie. I don't understand."

"You never had a boy like you just because?"

She picked her head off the table and shot me a wry glance. "Sure. All the time. In middle school."

"Well. I like you. In my thirties," I said.

"Say it again. I want to watch your lips when you say it. Say it slow and sexy."

"Slow and sexy," I said.

"I'm serious. Tell me you like me."

"And I like you. Just because I do."

"Mackenzie, I'm so aroused. Oh wow, okay, my turn, watch my lips. Watch the muscles of my mouth. I like you, too," she said. She had those lips that don't form a straight line, but rather bend and curve. The tip of her tongue pressed against her teeth when she pronounced "Like." "Mackenzie," she said, forming elongated syllables. "You can have me. For the night."

"You do this often with your dates?" I asked. "Because I dig it. I read it in a DeLillo book once."

"No, never tried it before. No one I respect has ever told me he likes me. Plus you've got the great jaw and full lips. Watch me again. I want you. Upstairs."

"Upstairs," I repeated.

"Now." Her mouth formed the word slowly and fully. "Take my clothes off. This instant."

I stood. Ronnie came into my arms and wrapped her legs around my waist. She wasn't heavy and I carried her upstairs. She kissed my cheek, my ear, my neck.

I fell backwards into bed. She sat astride my hips with the light on, and glanced at my belongings.

"As I predicted. Simple. Orderly. Masculine. You don't even have spare change on your nightstand. And books everywhere, I love books. And your bed is made. Who makes the bed? Nobody, that's who. Your drawers are closed and there's a basket of folded laundry waiting to be put away, and an ironing board, and I love everything about this room. I want to live here forever."

"Ronnie."

"Yes Mackenzie."

"Stop talking," I said.

"Yes Mackenzie. Turn off the reading lamp."

I did.

She tugged her shirt over her head, nothing underneath. Her skin had pale tan lines from a bikini, dainty triangles. She lowered her mouth to mine and we kissed for a long time.

We kissed until the wooden stairs squeaked. Someone in the hallway. I recognized the tread. Uh oh.

My bedroom door opened and light spilled over us. Her breath caught and she turned.

Manny tiptoed in and shut the door behind him. He couldn't see in the dark yet, blinded by hallway light. He stumbled on something, cursed, and lay down on my floor. He'd been drinking.

Ronnie turned back to me, eyes enormous.

She mouthed the words, What the hell!

I grinned. Sounds came from the floor, as he laid the gun under his pillow and pulled up the blanket.

She put her lips next to my ear. She didn't produce noise but I understood the words anyway.

Is that your gorgeous friend?

I nodded.

He sleeps in here?

I nodded again.

Kinky, she mouthed, and she wriggled suggestively.

I started to push myself up on my elbows. We had a spare bedroom, after all, and the need was great. She shoved me back and held a finger to her lips.

"It's okay. We can wait a few minutes," she said.

I nodded.

She pushed my shirt up to expose my chest. She lay down flat against me, her face on my skin, and let out a happy sigh.

I pulled the corner of the blanket up and covered her as best I could and her chest trembled with silent laughter. We lay, quietly, until Manny began a soft snore. Almost a feminine sound.

But it wasn't Manny.

It was my date. She was asleep.

25

Ronnie woke up at five. Her shoes were still on. I watched as she quietly hunted for her diaphanous spaghetti-strap shirt.

"Want breakfast?" I whispered.

She smiled and lowered to my ear again. "Another time. I know I owe you, and I'll make it up. 'Kay? I promise. You'll need breakfast then to get your strength back."

"The Rescue Mission is going to fire you, talking like that."

"Falling asleep was the happiest I've been in months. Great night. Can I wake up Kix? Just for snuggles?"

"No."

"I know." She kissed my forehead. "Bye."

She pulled on her shirt, gingerly stepped over Manny, waved, and fled.

At the breakfast table, Kix sat unusually still and scowled. Accusation was heavy in the air. His bananas and dry cereal were untouched.

"What?" I asked.

You know. He told me with his eyes. *You know.*

"Nothing happened," I said.

Kix grunted. And kept staring.

She's trouble. You know this.

"I know this. But I like her, Kix."

So? She's hiding secrets. She's a mess.

"She loves you," I said. "Thinks you're beautiful."

Obviously.

He picked up a piece of cereal and threw it at me. He missed. Hah. Small victories.

"No sir," I said. He did it again. "Kix. No."

You can't solve her problems, Father. You're on thin ice. Very thin ice.

"She likes me."

Gross.

"I know. Can't help it."

What do you think her secrets are? They won't be fun.

"I have guesses. An ex-husband, perhaps. Maybe she's broke. Maybe she's in counseling."

And you want to yolk yourself to that disaster? Come on, Dad. Beauty is vain.

"She's more than pretty. She's smart. And funny. And kind."

Gross again. Get a grip.

"You're right." I sat down and rested my chin on my hand, elbow propped on the table. "You're right. I know. It'd be the blind leading the blind. Can't I have some fun, though?"

He arched an eyebrow and picked up a piece of cereal.

You want another one of these? Think about what you're saying. I'll throw this, don't think I won't. What kind of girl comes to your house and starts crying? The wrong kind, that's who. How did your fun work out in Los Angeles? Did that fun end well?

"No. No, it didn't."

He ate the cereal.

I'm glad we had this chat.

"I'm not."

⟿

KEVIN WAS BACK AT SCHOOL, finally. The tall kid, sunken eyes, the one who'd attacked me. His suspension was over. He brought no books with him to class. No pencil, no pen. Never made eye contact and didn't respond. Glared at his desk for an hour. Great guy, bright future.

Jeriah sat behind Kevin and eyed him. He was worried. After class, Jeriah let all the other kids file out first. He stayed back. He was a good-sized kid, getting bigger through the shoulders.

"Mr. August, man, look. There's about to be problems," he said.

"Do tell."

"Kevin and some others think you're a cop."

I nodded. "I heard that rumor. I used to be, in California. No longer."

"Yeah. Well. Kevin and his buddies, they plan on jumping you."

"Jumping me," I said.

"Yeah, you know? Knock the shit out you."

"Is Kevin in a gang?"

"Think so," Jeriah said. "We aren't friends like we used to be. He quit talking."

"Thanks for the warning, Jeriah."

"What are you going to do?"

"Right now? Teach second period."

"No, Mr. August, I mean, about Kevin and his buddies? They're going to fight you," he said.

"I'll encourage them to stop."

"I know you're a big dude, but." He shook his head and shoved his hands into his jacket pockets. "Could end up hurt."

"Oh no. And I bruise like a peach, too."

"What?"

"Nothing." I clapped him on the shoulder. "Thanks, Jeriah. I'll be careful."

He walked out, and only then did I notice Megan. The girl in tortoise-shell glasses who sat in the front row and made all As. She clutched books to her chest and waited.

"Can I help you, Megan?"

"Please don't get hurt," she said. "You're my favorite teacher."

"Extra credit for you, my dear, because of your superb judge in character."

In the hallway, Reginald Willis was hollering, "Run along, now, little ones, run along! You men with your young healthy prostates need no bathroom break! Move it! Leave the virtuous ladies alone. We have work we must be about, and it doesn't involve chasing skirts! These girls are too much trouble, anyway. Focus on your studies! On your books! Run along!"

"BRYCE HARPER IS NOT worth four hundred million," I said. Manny and I sat on the front porch, drinking Coronas. Nine o'clock and all was well. The beetles and cicadas had dimmed with the coming of milder temperatures.

"Yes he is! El burro sabe mas que tu, estúpido. He plays a hundred sixty games a year."

"In his first five seasons in the bigs, he had one good year. One." I held up my pointer finger for illustrative purposes.

"He got the MVP that year," Manny said.

"And I love him for it. I'd like to see him string together two or three excellent seasons before shelling out four hundred million. Dollars, not pesos."

"People pay to watch him play, Mack. He's my favorite white person."

"Don't use my first name. Ever. And baseball players aren't like football or basketball. They don't have the same star power. Was Alex Rodriguez worth those contracts? No way."

He held up his middle finger, for offensive purposes. "Sorry, Mack. You're wrong, Mack."

"I'm reporting you to immigration."

"I'm a marshal. And I'm thinking 'bout arresting you. You resist and I'll shoot your pinky."

"Real men don't have pinkies."

He shook his head.

"Where's Ronnie? I want to look at that mamita. Just look, you know? Brings me life."

"I do know. But I'm not sure about her, Manuel. She's got baggage."

"Qué? What kind?"

"She won't tell me."

"You like her?" he asked.

"Yeah. I do."

"I'll tail her. Investigate."

"No," I said. "That's bananas."

"She got baggage? I'll find out. I'm sneaky."

"No."

"Want me to bug her apartment?" he asked.

"Noooooooooo, Manny. Listen to my words."

"I'll put cameras. In her shower."

"You have deep issues."

My phone rang. Didn't recognize the number, but I answered.

"This is Mackenzie."

"Mr. August, this is Marcus Morgan, Jeriah's father. Listen quick. Jeriah has informed me that his friend Kevin is on his way to your house, with malicious intent."

"Uh oh," I said.

"Do me a favor. Lock your doors and don't call 911. I'm on the way. I know Kevin and his friends and I'll talk sense."

"I can talk sense, too, Marcus. No need for you to rush over."

"I'm on the way." He hung up.

I looked at Manny, who drained his beer. "About to have company."

"Who?" he asked.

"Local high schoolers. They have a grudge."

His face split into a smile. "Your class is coming to beat up their teacher?"

"Manny. Don't take this as a referendum on my teaching ability."

"Wow," he said. "You must really suck."

"That is not the appropriate lens through which to view this situation. Instead, consider them challengers to my King of the Hill status."

He stood and stretched, stepped off the porch, and wandered into the privacy pines along the side of our property. The pistol grip pressed against his shirt above the belt.

I stayed in my rocking chair.

A minute later an old Chevy Malibu pulled into view and parked a block away. Four doors open, four doors closed. Four figures walked under the streetlight and approached my yard. It was like they wore a uniform - white Nikes, baggy jeans slung low, and T-shirts decorated with red.

I heard a voice say, "I dunno, man, let's just go," and I recognized that it belonged to Kevin.

"We here. We doing this. C'mon."

I spoke up.

"Evening, gents."

The four silhouettes froze on the walk leading to my steps.

"Shit. He's on the porch."

"Yes," I agreed. "Yes he is."

Kevin hung in the back, shoulders slumped, hands in his pockets. I didn't know the other three, who were older than Kevin. Wonder how they knew where I lived?

Short guy in the front barked, "You a cop."

"You is wrong. I teach. I used to be a detective, in Los Angeles," I said. "No longer. Want to come inside? For a lemonade?"

"C'mon," Kevin said in a low grunt. "This is stupid. Let's leave."

Another voice, "Shut up. Knew you'd pussy out."

"He ain't worth it."

"I'm not," I said. "Kevin's right. I'm not worth it. You should go home."

The leader of the gang of four, the shortest and stockiest, approached my porch. In addition to the sneakers/jeans/red t-shirt combo, he wore a White Sox cap. What an idiot. He bent down to retrieve one of my heavy decorative Mexican beach pebbles I kept around the peonies. He played catch with it.

"Come here, old man," he said.

"Put down my rock, please."

"Or what?"

"Or I'll take it."

He played catch with one hand, and with the other he retrieved a pistol from his front pocket. Front pocket? Those were big jeans. The pistol didn't gleam, making me think it was a small caliber Glock.

"Bitch, I'mma take turns throwing rocks at'cha ass and shooting, till you come down here."

I stood. I came down the front stairs.

"Now what?" I said.

I was bigger than he expected. A foot taller almost, and twice as wide, and he lost a bit of bravado. He was never going to shoot me. Bullying and fighting are a lot different than murder, but the gun made me nervous.

"*Big* white man," he said.

"Put my rock down now. And how about that lemonade?"

"So you a cop?"

"No sir, I'm not."

"I been hearing stories," he said. "Stories don't make me happy."

"Who are you?"

"Just a black man, telling you to watch your step. Unner-stand?"

"No name? I'll call you Shorty."

His friends snickered. Kevin looked unhappy.

I continued, "Make me stop? Stop what?"

"You call me Shorty again, I'll kill you. You get it?"

"I need to know what I'm supposed to stop," I said.

"You doing more than teach."

"Like what?"

"Know what's good for you, you'll back off," he said.

"Back off what?"

"You know."

"No, I don't. What should I stop doing?"

"Fuck you," said Shorty, because he didn't know what else to say. Shorty was stuck. He'd been sent by someone, but he didn't know why. He hadn't been told because the sender didn't want me to know. These cop rumors were originating somewhere. I wanted to know where.

Kevin said, "Okay, time to go. We told him. C'mon guys."

I said, "You know nothing, Shorty. Just an errand boy."

Shorty took a swing at me with the rock. Such a pathetic move. He telegraphed the motion, like a quarterback with a slow windup and release. It has to be fast, one motion, pow, to have any effect.

I knocked his rock hand down, like I might do with Kix, and he staggered off balance. I got his gun hand in my fist and bent it backwards.

Shorty cried out in pain. I had my thumb over the hammer, which meant it wasn't a Glock.

"Kevin, go to the sidewalk," I said. "I know for a fact you have homework."

The other two guys suddenly had guns also.

Crud.

I wrenched Shorty's hand, breaking or badly spraining it, and removed the gun. I did it quickly, giving me time to shove his closest buddy backwards. Hard, driving from my shoulder. He fell. Bought me two seconds.

That left Kevin. And the other guy with a gun. Aimed at me.

Suddenly Manny was there. He used his pistol to hit the third guy in the back of the skull, a savage blow. Like breaking a melon. The guy dropped.

Three men down.

Manny pointed his gun at Kevin.

"No," I said. "Manny, don't point that at him."

Kevin was pale and breathing heavy. His hands were in the air.

Shorty was groaning and holding his wrist.

"We're good, Manny," I said. "We're good."

Manny walked to the kid I'd shoved to the ground. The kid still had a revolver in his hand. Manny put one boot on the gun and with the other boot he kicked the kid in the face. Busted his lip. Kicked again. And again.

"You don't come here with guns," Manny said, and he had a scary cold hissing note to his voice. "You never bring guns to a man's house. You comprende that?"

"Kevin, go home," I said. "Okay? Go home."

Kevin's hands were still up and he couldn't move. Kevin's life was much more real and harsh than it had been an hour ago. A further loss of innocence. Maybe it was good he learned now.

Manny quit kicking and took away the kid's revolver.

I collected Shorty's gun, a cheap .38. Felt plastic. I also took the fourth gun from the grass, next to the kid Manny had surprised.

Pistols everywhere.

"Shit," Kevin whimpered.

Manny inserted the barrel of his Glock 22 into Shorty's mouth. Shorty cried and twisted, but Manny held him still.

"Manny," I said. "They're kids. Ease up."

Manny's face was close to Shorty's, and he was sweating. On the verge of madness. "You're a tough guy," Manny said. He moved the pistol around inside Shorty's mouth, clicking against his teeth, and Shorty was crying. "But not really. You're a little boy, playing with grown men. I've seen Mackenzie break a man's teeth. For fun. You get that?"

A car was speeding down the street. Kevin looked torn. He wanted to run but couldn't.

With his other hand Manny cocked the revolver, the pistol taken from the kid he kicked. He pressed the revolver into Shorty's groin. Shorty had a barrel in the mouth and another in the balls. If this didn't scare him straight, nothing would, poor bastard.

"Pow," he said, and Shorty spasmed in fear. "You come here again and I'll shoot your dick off. Comprende? Done it before, and I'll do it again."

The car was a Lexus. An LS, the big one. It squealed to a stop, the front tire on my sidewalk.

Marcus Morgan got out and left it running. "Whoa, whoa! Everyone relax. Be cool. Kevin! Get into my car. Right now, Kevin."

He had a good voice, full of iron and anger. Kevin didn't hesitate. He almost ran to the car.

Marcus came into the yard and said, "Shit. What happened?"

"The boys were playing with guns," I said. "We couldn't wait for you."

Manny stood up. He had a gun in each fist. I did too. Marcus eyed us warily. "You two did this?"

Manny was still angry. Big breaths coming through his nostrils. "You are who?"

"Manny, this is Marcus Morgan. Marcus called to warn about the boys and their toys. Marcus, this is my good friend Manuel. I think we can all calm down now."

"How the hell did you do this? Four boys with guns? You two don't have a scratch."

"They're kids," I said. "We're not."

"You've done it before?"

"We have," I said.

Marcus walked to all three boys and told them to get in the car, like a father scolding little kids. They obeyed, slowly and in various states of pain.

"Kid with the busted-up mouth, I don't even know that one," Marcus said. Then he hollered at them, "You get blood on my car, I'll kill you."

"You know the other three?" I asked.

"And their mothers. This will be a long night for them boys. You see, Mr. August? It takes a village."

"And sometimes an ass kicking."

Marcus said, "Or sometimes ten. I appreciate you not phoning the police. That'd only make it worse. Boys pretending to be something they're not. You guys sure you're okay?"

"Positive. Need another beer, though. Calm the nerves."

"If you want, I'll deliver the pistols to the police station," he said.

"Nah," Manny said. "I'll handle it."

"Are you a police officer?"

"Something like that. Time for you to go, hombre, because I'm still a little jumpy."

"Sure. Yeah, sure. I get that. Damn, what a mess."

"Tell Jeriah thanks," I said.

"I will. Definitely. Thanks again, gentlemen. I hope the rest of your night is peaceful."

The Lexus LS dropped into drive and motored down the street. We could hear Marcus yelling within.

"Those assholes don't know the rules," Manny said. "Never make it personal. You don't go to a man's home."

"Technically, Manny, I think you're homeless."

"Qué? No, señor, this is my home too."

"Mi casa es su casa?" I asked.

"Sí."

"Then you should pay rent, hombre," I said.

"Don't I pay rent? I should."

"You should."

"Maybe I will," he said.

"And maybe sleep in your own room?"

"Don't be silly, estúpido. I like the floor."

26

I hadn't seen Eddie Backpack in days. I stood in the hallway and scrutinized the flood but he simply wasn't there. Chances were, he'd gotten spooked. Told Big Will that teachers got suspicious, and transferred to a different school and now Big Will arranged other suppliers to infiltrate Patrick Henry. That was my guess.

My two leads now were Trevor and Big Will.

And Kevin, but he'd skipped school today. I didn't blame him. That would have been awkward.

My cover was most likely blown. Kevin and the gang of four would relate the story to others, and more rumors would start, and blah blah.

Mackenzie August, major league screwup.

~

THAT NIGHT DAD and I ate steak and salad, and Kix worked on small pieces of pear and a bottle. Dad had Frank Sinatra playing from the Bose stereo on the counter.

"Manny told me about last night," he said. "I didn't even notice the fracas, so immersed I was in a book."

"Which book?"

"*Just Mercy*. Really eye-opening. I think I may be a bit of a racist. But I'm working on it."

"Lecherous, Timothy, the word is lecherous."

He wiped his mouth with a napkin and sat back. "Here's what I want to know. And I'm only curious because Manny is curious."

"Okay."

"The boy, Kevin," Timothy August said. "From last night. Manny said you were worried only about him. Go home, Kevin. Don't shoot Kevin. Stuff like that."

"I am merciful and fearsome and mysterious."

"Is Kevin black?"

"Yes," I said. "They all were."

"Is he younger than the others?"

"A little."

"So is that why?" he asked.

"No. Kevin's in my class. I got a soft spot for him."

"Would you have a soft spot for the others? If they were your students?"

"Maybe." I shrugged. "Good question. But they're not my students, and I have no relationship with them. Ergo, keep Kevin alive."

"How is your investigation going, otherwise?"

"I've developed leads. I think my time might be up soon at Patrick Henry, and I'll pass along what I got."

"You've only been there a month," he said.

"But they caught on quick. Lots of rumors circulating about me, and not the good kind like how great my chicken cacciatore is."

"How did they guess your true occupation?" he asked.

"I don't know. Suspicious, though, isn't it? Like someone was working against us."

"Perhaps the assistant principal, the women you said made veiled threats."

"She's sometimes shrewish, but I doubt it. An administrator's life is hard enough as it is, and I'm not doing a bad job. But. Possibly her."

"You realize, son, that even if you are successful in your mission you won't stop the drugs. Nor even make a dent in them," he said.

"I know this. Teacher across the hall agrees with you."

"Then why do it?"

"It's never been about the drugs," I said.

"I don't understand."

"See? Mysterious and fearsome."

"Explain?" he asked.

"It's about teenage girls being hurt. And it's about a guy."

"Ah yes, a guy, the General."

"We can't eliminate all vices. We can't remove all temptations. Can't solve all problems. But perhaps we can do something about the worst of the worst. And I think this guy's it. Sheriff Stackhouse believes so."

"The pictures of the girls put you over the edge, I believe," he said.

"Probably. And..."

"And?"

"This is our city. Not his," I said. "It's a good place. And he's messing it up."

"You are as noble hearted as ever."

"And fearsome."

"My questions have all been answered. Thank you for the explanation."

"I am a faithful and obedient son," I said.

"That you are." He stood and washed his plate. "I'm going out for drinks. Back late."

"With a woman?"

"Drinks with a woman, yes."

"You are a faithful and wretched womanizer," I said.

"Honor your parents. That's in the Ten Commandments, right? Act like it."

"Yes sir. Enjoy your adultery," I said.

"I shall do my best."

∾

MANNY CAME HOME a few minutes later. He read two books to Kix, who tolerated Manny more with each day, put the kid to bed, opened a beer and sat down on the couch.

I glanced at my watch.

"You staying here for the rest of the night?" I asked.

"Simon."

"Simon?"

"Pronounced 'seeMOAN.' Means yup, en español."

"I'm going out for a few. If someone tries to take Kix—"

"I'll shoot 'em in the ass," Manny said.

"Simon."

I took off my sneakers and put on topsiders and a sports jacket and tucked my Kimber .45 into my belt.

Bond. James Bond.

Looking for Will. Big Will.

I was unusually nervous as I approached and parked next to the Addisonian Social Club. It was, as the kids say, lit. Big Will's truck was on the street. I sat in my car and watched the foot traffic until nine.

It would be hard to be a minority, I decided. For a lot of reasons, but also because fewer people looked like you. A simple but powerful factor. I became acutely aware of my whiteness as I noted eighteen of the twenty partiers plunging into the club weren't white. We're all racists, so said the Wall Street Journal, but I'd like to think I was less so than most and yet I still felt the tension of looking different.

I'm deeply profound.

I got out of my car, fastened the coat's top button, and walked to the entrance.

The Addisonian was, above all things, a fun place to be. Colors flashed, music played, and partiers danced. The ceiling was high and the lights were low, and balloons drifted on strings at the walls. Looked like two birthdays being celebrated. The Addisonian didn't have a traditional bar, but rather a communal kitchen stuffed with food and drink. Bring your own, I guessed, was the rule, to keep costs down.

There was not a bouncer, but two gentlemen near the door took on the role unofficially. I got an amused once-over.

"Damn man, you're a big dude," one guy shouted over the noise. He had on a gray t-shirt strained to the point of bursting with muscle. Khakis and work boots.

"Almost ten pounds at birth," I noted with pride. "Thanks for noticing."

"Who you here to see?"

"Just passing through," I said. "Open party?"

"Yep. Better if you know someone here."

"Reginald Willis told me about the place."

"You know Reginald?" he asked.

"Sure. Love Reggie. Talks my ear off about how I need to shave more."

Gray T-shirt's glower cracked and he chuckled good-naturedly. "Yeah, sounds like Reggie. He ain't here."

"Still. I am footloose and fancy free."

"Yeah, sure, man, up to you."

I found a corner and surveyed the scene. Because I'm an investigator, and because I cannot dance. To my trained eye, one thing became apparent; the people at the Addisonian had more fun than I did on my couch, most nights. And the women dressed better than Manny, and displayed more cleavage.

Big Will wasn't dancing either. He sat at a table with a red Solo cup and a collection of curvy woman and stout men. The men were overly serious and their dates talked at an overly loud decibel. I could watch and take notes and snap a few candid photographs with my camera for research later, like the intrepid detective I am. Much to my chagrin, though, Big Will was staring straight at me.

Drat. Thwarted. Should have worn a fake mustache.

Big Will spoke quietly to the man sitting to his left. That man rose and approached my corner.

He arrived and said, "Come with me."

"My, what big teeth you have."

"What?"

"Nothing. Lead on."

I followed him to Big Will's table. Another man got up and indicated I should "Spread 'em." I did and he patted me down.

"Pistol in the back," I said.

Big Will waved it away, and his man sat.

Regrettably there was no extra chair for me. He and his friends stared like I was a zoo animal. No one offered me theirs.

"Oh it's awkward. One sec."

I found a cushioned straight-back chair, brought it to Big Will, and sat next to him. Not at the table, but close enough.

"Ahh, that's better. Now it's not awkward," I said.

Big Will still had the grizzly beard and shaved head, reminding me of James Harden, the NBA point guard. His biceps and thighs bulged like tree trunks. He picked up his cup and drank once.

"I'm not happy." He had a soft, high-pitched way of speaking. I'm not sure what I expected, maybe a bawling sailor. "Not happy to see your ugly ass here. This is a good place."

"You know me."

"I do. What do you want."

"I want Bryce Harper to play for the Nationals till he's forty-five, for fifteen million a year."

"What?"

"It'll never happen, I know, but we can dream."

"You should not be here," Big Will said.

"You just invited me."

"Not to this table, motherfucker, to this place. This is a good place. No troubles."

"I brought no troubles with me. I am affronted by the suggestion. I came to dance."

"Look like a cop," he said.

"I'm not a cop. I'm a teacher."

"Big damn teacher. Packing heat," he said.

"You look like James Harden, but I'm not giving you grief. If you are? I think you should pass more."

"James Harden's a punk," he said. "Westbrook tear his ass up.

Look. I don't know what's going on. And maybe I don't gotta know. But there's business and there's personal. We are relaxing." He put the emphasis on "-laxing," drawing it out. "We got kids. We got women. This ain't the place."

"I get that. But, how do you know me?"

"We know you. Smart-ass cop, feeling out the local distribution. You should be ass up in the ground but you ain't, because I'm nice. And then you show up here."

I had a sneaking and very definite suspicion that my cover was blown. That somehow all of my elite clandestine surveillance work had been discovered, and instead of me getting the drop on them, the tables had been turned.

Lesser men would be daunted.

I was simply confused.

He said, "We tryna be tolerant of you, but you on my nerves now. I see you again, I'll kill you and deal with repercussions later."

"Can I feel your muscles?" I said.

"Keep it up, asshole, see what happens."

"You're the boss?"

"I'm your boss, and that's all that matters."

"Who's your boss?" I asked.

"Don't got one."

"Ah, but see, you referenced repercussions earlier. The boss is implied, and he or she mentioned me. Tell me who it is and I'll put in a good word for you. Get that Christmas bonus."

Big Will indicated two of his friends and said, "This is Ray. And this is Echo. They will walk you to the door. You don't leave immediately and they'll break your fingers."

"But I need those."

Ray and Echo stood, big fellows, and so did I.

"Suppose I'm a little outnumbered," I said.

"Damn right."

"What's your number?" I said. "I'll call you."

Ray and Echo closed in.

"Never mind. I'll get it from Ray. So long, Big Will."

I walked to the door. So did Ray and Echo. I left behind the music and laughter and walked down the sidewalk. So did Ray and Echo.

"Nice evening," I said.

"Yup."

"You guys gonna walk me all the way to my car?"

"Yup."

"Okay, over here." I jogged across the street.

They followed.

"Wait. I didn't park over here," I said. "Silly me."

I jogged back the way I came. They followed.

"Oh, no, my mistake. I was right the first time."

I jogged across the street *again*. They followed, reluctantly and a bit peeved.

"Hmm. Not here. Simon says, let's go back and check the other side again," I said, and I crossed the street a fourth time. The two quasi-bouncers at the bar watched this with deep concern and bemusement.

Ray and Echo reached my side of the street, panting just a bit.

"Still not here," I said. "Should we go check for my car on the other side again? Simon says?"

"Okay, asshole, we get it. Just leave. Okay?" Ray said.

"Yeah sure. You guys on Facebook? Hit me up."

Ray and Echo returned to the Addisonian.

27

"Life ain't easy, boys and girls!" Reginald Willis bawled. "Who told you it was? Lies! You work hard and maybe one day you won't be poor! Until then, you poor! Poor in spirit, poor in cash, poor in character, and only hard work can save you! You want to watch television the rest of your life? How about you, young lady, you planning on a career of staring at your phone? At Netflix? No ma'am! That ain't the way!"

The bell rang. Class began.

No Kevin.

I asked Megan, the girl in the front row, "Was Kevin here yesterday?"

"I don't think so, Mr. August."

"He came late!" Jeriah shouted from the back. "Skipped this class. 'Fraid to look at'cha, Mr. August. Hah!"

"Text him. Tell him to get his ass back to my class," I said.

"Mr. August...you can't say that."

"Oh, sorry, Megan, you're right. Jeriah, tell him I said please. Where are my manners. Happy, Megan?"

"No."

"Yeah, me neither at the moment."

AFTER SCHOOL IN THE TEACHERS' parking lot, an enormous black truck loomed beside my humble Honda. Shiny and intimidating. To lesser men.

Nate Silva buzzed the driver's window down.

"Hey teacher. Get in."

"I'm not sure I can," I said. "Do you have a stepladder?"

He buzzed the window back up. Rude.

I went around, climbed into the passenger's seat, and closed the door. The spacious cabin smelled like strong cologne, and the pine-scented air freshener hanging from his rearview, and marijuana. The aroma of weed always made me sleepy.

He had a gun in his left fist, but it didn't scare me. He couldn't shoot someone sitting in his passenger seat on school grounds, and this parking lot had electronic surveillance.

"You about finished?" Silva asked. He wore jeans and a leather jacket, red T-shirt underneath. His head was freshly shorn.

"With the latest Stuart Woods book? No, haven't started. What's that rascal Stone up to now?"

"The hell you talking about?"

"I'm being witty," I said, although it should have been obvious.

"This is done. It's over. You get it? *Finito.*"

"What are we talking about, Silva?"

"You poking your nose into my business. That's what. And it's over," he said.

"What is your business?"

"My business is my business."

"Maybe you should ask politely," I said.

"I asked politely the other night."

"You send kids to do your scary work?" I asked.

"Next time I won't."

It's hard to sit in a truck cab and glare sideways at each other but we were doing it.

"Don't come back to my house," I said.

"Do I need to?"

"That's not how this works. You send more guys to my house, I won't play nice. I'll break their noses and their arms, yeah, but I'll kill you. You want to be a professional? Learn the rules."

"Ain't no rules in the jungle. But I don't need to come to your house. I can make you stop by using alternate means," he said.

"Alternate means? Holy smokes, Silva, can you read too? Them's big words. And what is this alternative? Tickle fight?"

"You're good, August. I get it. You beat me in that fake fight. You used to be a big shot in Los Angeles. I get it. Okay, motherfucker? I get it. But here, you're playing with fire. You ain't as slick as you think. You been seen. Anytime you come round, we see you."

More teachers came into the parking lot. Laughing. Hurrying home. The big black truck got a few second glances.

"I hear the Bloods got themselves a general," I said and his expression visibly darkened. He pursed his lips and his eyes narrowed. "And I hear he's good. That you?"

"That's me."

"No it's not, Silva. You're small potatoes."

"Stay alive, Teach. Your boy needs a dad. Go back to the lawyer business," Silva said.

"Would you mind if I recorded this conversation? So I can remember it all?"

"You show up to work tomorrow, it's war. You tell anyone about me, it's war."

"What the hell do I tell them, Silva? Watch out for the ugly guy in the big black truck because he'll tell you to stop doing vague things that piss him off?"

"Don't show up to work tomorrow," he said.

"I'm going to."

"Take a sick day."

"No," I said, and pulled on the handle to open the door. "Assistant Principal Deere would be angry with me, and she's terrifying. See you tomorrow."

MANNY CAME into the kitchen triumphant that evening. Triumph, on his chiseled face, was quite a sight.

I had chili cooking on the stove and Kix watched Sesame Street. An old episode. The guest was Tina Fey.

"Qué onda, cabrón. I tailed your chica," he announced.

"That better be Spanish for 'I need a nap.'"

"I followed Ronnie the whole day," he said.

"I asked you not to."

"Yeah. Well."

"For this you are employed by taxpayers?" I asked. "Seems fiscally irresponsible of America."

"You want to know? What she did?"

"I do not," I said.

"Yes you do."

"You're correct. I do. Tell me."

He rotated the chair and sat, so that his legs straddled the back. He tapped on his phone a few times, cleared his throat theatrically, and said, "I present to you...La Historia de Ronnie."

"Want a beer?"

"No. Shush. Her real name is Veronica Summers. Did you know this?"

"I did," I said.

"No you didn't. Shush. Veronica Summers rises early. She was at Golds Gym off Electric by five-thirty in the morning. She participated in a hot yoga class and came home without showering."

"You're not a member of Golds, Manny. How'd you get in?"

"I smiled at the girl at the desk."

"Ah," I said. The chili needed more tomatoes so I diced another half on the cutting board. "You used the force."

"And if the girl at the desk texts me, I may visit her bedroom. Because that señorita got ass. But I digress. Did I say that correctly? Digress. Ronnie was back at her place by seven, and then out again at seven forty-five."

"Less than forty-five minutes for shower and makeup," I noted. "Doesn't leave much time for prep work."

"Girl doesn't take much to look crazy fly, hombre," Manny pointed out.

"That barn don't need painting."

"What?"

"Nada. Carry on."

"She drove a red Mercedes C-Class to her office, which is off Campbell. Second floor, windows in the back. She stayed there until noon, at which point she lunched alone at The Quarter. A friend or business associate stopped to talk during the final five minutes. The friend would be pretty, if she wasn't eating with Veronica Summers. You dig?"

"I dig," I said.

"I got a photo. Wanna view?"

"I do not."

"Back at the office by one. A lone hombre visited at two. Came with an iPad. Wore a cheap suit. I got a photo. Drove a Toyota, license registered to Fredrick Wheeler. I looked him up, because I am intelligente, and he is a lawyer out of Harrisonburg."

I said, "Let's assume that is work related. Does she have a receptionist?"

"Sí, Natasha Gordon, and Natasha went home a quarter till four. Ronnie went for drinks at Billy's. People like her, want to talk with her, but for the most part she preferred to drink alone in the corner, and she talked with the bartender. The bartender's name is Carrie. Ronnie left for home alone at five. Still there when I left."

"So, Manuel my suspicious Mexican, we're no closer to solving the mystery of her secrets. And thusly, I think, we should leave it."

"Not so fast, maestro. First, I was born in Buenos Aires, Argentina. And second, I went back to her office after five. An hour ago."

"I don't want to hear anymore."

"Yes you do," Manny said. "Her office is locked up tighter than Fort Knox. Comprende? Two independent security systems, including one monitored remotely. Bars in the windows. Cameras."

"Ah hah!"

"Ah hah, what?"

"A clue," I said.

"I wonder what she keeps in there, jefe."

"You didn't find out?"

"No, señor," he said.

"What does America pay you for?"

"I shoot people in the ass."

THAT NIGHT I lay in bed, staring at my iPhone. I'd typed out a text to Sheriff Stackhouse twice. And deleted it twice.

What would I tell her?

Nate Silva told me to go away?

Some high school kids are angry with me?

There may or may not be drugs at a warehouse off Shenandoah?

A guy named Big Will scares Reginald?

There's a kid named Eddie who will deny everything?

Put it all together, and it gives the appearance of significance. But take it apart and each piece of the whole is thin. Nothing conclusive. And worst of all, they'd figured me out. Almost immediately, so it appeared, and that aggravated me. Was I so clumsy?

I'd done a bad job. No other way to look at it. Now I wanted to run to the police? I'm no amateur. No wimp.

I wanted to piss off Silva. He'd sent kids to my house, he'd pulled a gun on me. I'd go to work tomorrow and see what happened. He promised a war. Now he'd have to deliver. Chances were, though, it'd been a bluff.

Come get me, Silva.

Or Ronnie, she could come get me. Either one.

28

My car didn't blow up - I checked first, to be safe, in the morning.

No one followed me to Roxanne's to deliver Kix. And no one shot me as I pulled into school.

I made copies in the office. The receptionists talked into their phones. Ms. Deere's heels clicked up the hall and Reginald Willis hummed in his classroom. The custodian was peeling gum off a water fountain. All seemed well. Students soon flooded the halls, same as always.

Pretty boring war.

First period began. Megan noted, "Mr. August, Kevin is missing again."

"I see that. Jeriah? Any word from our boy?"

"No sir, he don't tell me nothing," Jeriah said. He looked concerned.

The wimp.

∾

RONNIE TEXTED me during my planning period.

\>> **Hey handsome stranger**

\>> **There's a hockey game tonight**

\>> **First game of the season!**

\>> **Meet me at Berglunds Civic Center?**

\>> **I've got good seats**

I was a man who lived by principles. I paid my taxes and took multivitamins. I ate veggies and avoided gluttony. Rarely was I drunk. I'd read books on how to be a better father. I got enough exercise, and went to bed early as often as I could. I was patriotic and went to church and believed in Jesus and had no debt.

And I didn't date women like Veronica Summers. She was mysterious, while I wanted an open book life. She disappeared for days and claimed she had secrets and sins I could never discover. She had family trauma she wouldn't discuss.

And yet. I wanted her. Ronnie was fun and friendly and she read books to kids. She had a law degree and she mixed drinks. She adored my house and my son. She thought I was handsome, and I thought she was the prettiest human being I'd ever seen in real life.

Dating her was going to involve pain. Lots of misery.

But maybe some girls are worth it?

Probably couldn't figure this out while I grade papers, huh. A lesser man would cower and hide, but not I.

I texted her back.

Should I pick you up?

\>> **Even better.**

\>> **Afterwards, back to your place.**

\>> **To the guest bedroom this time.**

\>> **For third date bliss.**

\>> **I owe you. >=) =P**

∾

RONNIE WORE EMBROIDERED white trousers which gathered above the ankle, peep-toe heels with no backs, and a long-sleeve Henley because, "It gets cold, of course." Her hair hung loose and straight, not thick, not thin, the texture that shimmers in waves like silk. She looked so healthy, so happy, so fit and full of life that folks on the sidewalk stopped to watch her get into my car. I gave them the "I know, right, how'd she get so lucky?" eyebrow arch.

"Gosh you smell good," she said, and her fingers found mine. "Good enough to eat."

"I smell like corndog nuggets?"

"Why are you wearing a sports coat?" she asked.

So it'll hide my pistol, because I don't trust Silva.

"Because it gets cold, of course," I said.

She pinched me.

A man waving a flashlight cone directed us to a parking spot near the back of the Civic Center lot. I turned off the ignition and Ronnie grabbed my coat and pulled me close. She kissed me hard and aggressive. Her fingers found my shirt buttons, released the top two, and slid inside.

"We're going to be tardy," I noted from the corner of my mouth.

"We can be late," she breathed. "It's hockey. Who cares?"

"Not I."

We missed the first period, but made it in time to start the second. The air inside the area was chilled and electric, the sensation live sports provided. Her seats were next to the glass, close enough that we ducked when pucks connected. The announcer and horn were loud and the crowd enthusiastic, and our team was winning 2-0. I ordered us each a hot pretzel and beer, and Ronnie beat on the glass during a fight, and for twenty minutes life was good.

Between periods we sat down and she rested her head on my shoulder, her hand around my bicep.

"Are you working with Brad Thompson Law right now?" she asked. "On anything fun?"

"No, I'm on a full-time assignment. No time for Brad at the moment."

"What's the case?" she asked.

"Drug trafficking. I'm helping locate some of the larger players."

She sat up, amusement and confusion bright in her face. "How on earth are you doing that? Undercover?"

"Kinda. I used to teach English, and the sheriff asked me to do it again this year, and collect information from the inside. The school's infested."

"So you're a high school English teacher?"

I nodded. We had to speak loudly over the hockey arena din.

"Currently. If I survive the year."

"And you accepted the position to help the police identify and arrest drug traffickers?" she asked.

I nodded again.

"Correct. Don't tell anyone. Or the students will murder me."

She nodded slightly and turned her attention back to the game.

But I'd lost her. Something went awry, and her expression grew distant. There was another fight on the ice but she didn't stand. Our team netted a goal but she didn't notice. She could have been on the other side of the planet. With five minutes left, she excused herself and pushed past me. Trying not to cry.

I gave her a ten second head start and followed.

She went straight for the doors, reached the parking lot, and began walking in the opposite direction of my car.

"Ronnie," I said.

She didn't turn. Didn't stop.

I followed.

"Ronnie," I said again when we reached the edge of the cars. Just beyond her, traffic roared on Williamson. She paused, a shadow framed by passing headlights. "You've got a lot going on inside. Be healthier if you shared."

"I'm breaking up with...me," she said. Her voice was high and choked.

"Why?"

"Why? Because. Because everything. Because you're a teacher and you're working to catch drug traffickers and your father loves you and you're a good dad and you haven't forced yourself on me and a thousand other reasons which prove I'm not good enough for you. I can't break up with *you* because you're a complete person, a decent human, and I'm lucky you haven't realized I'm human filth, so I'm doing your job for you," she said. Her words bordered on hysteria.

"You're operating under a lot of guilt, Ronnie. Take a deep breath and release some of the judgement. You're crushing yourself."

"I wish I hadn't met you." She paced back and forth, three steps, one two three turn, one two three turn, holding her left arm with her right hand. "Before, I thought my life was okay. Now, I realize it's bull. One big lie, you know?"

"I don't know," I said. "Tell me."

"Girls like me don't get guys like you. Girls like me marry gross men with money, divorce several times, have kids who hate them, get plastic surgery and look fake and shitty, and make money at jobs we don't enjoy until we die of lung cancer at sixty. And the whole time we're with the rich gross men we wish he was the cute honest boy, the boy named Mackenzie August. But he saw I was broken years ago, and he married the woman of his dreams, and he's faithful to her, and her kids love her, and she has friends who sit on beaches with her, and it's a fucking fairy tale, but I'll be at home drinking alone and wondering where *everyone* is."

"So you're nothing more than a stereotype? That's horse shit," I said. I'd covered half the distance between us. "Women like that don't read at the Rescue Mission."

"I thought I could fake it. I want to be a better person, I want to be the kind of girl who marries boys like you, the girl who won't eventually be exposed and embarrassed, but I can't. It's exhausting pretending. I can't sleep, can't eat."

"I'm lost, Ronnie. These secrets of yours, they can't go on."

"I'm engaged, Mackenzie. I'm getting married next year. His name is Brent and he is a federal prosecutor living in Washington DC. and he's rich and his parents are well-connected, and all that shit." With each word her spirit shrunk until she looked broken and small.

I hadn't guessed this. My head swam. I never saw a ring or a tan line. My ears were hot and I felt raw.

"Do you love him?" I asked.

"Who cares? You are worlds removed from my reality, Mackenzie. Your father loves you and supported you even when you moved to California."

It had begun to rain, intermittent fat drops splattering the windshields.

"My father?" she said. "My father arranged the marriage. My father and fiancé make me work at a bar on Friday nights to keep me busy, so I can't have a social life. Can you blame them? I practically undress every time I see you."

I stopped advancing. Because when I did she took little steps backwards, closer to busy Williamson.

"That's where you went? When you left for a week?"

"I had a lot of stuff to do, but I visited him, yes. He and my father both have friendly informants in the building where I live, and they get updates, and that's why I didn't let you in. Same with my office. And if I protest, my father can be cruel," she said.

This was deep water and I was over my head. Clearly she was an adult, and she didn't need to follow through with an arranged marriage or put up with an abusive father, but family is tricky, and I couldn't provide years of counseling in a parking lot. She wasn't speaking rationally, possibly due to a lifetime of abuse. I scrambled for any words that might bring about a positive conclusion to this conversation, but nothing came.

"You're a terrible feminist," I noted.

"Family is family. Even when they aren't. So you see," she half laughed, half sobbed, "why you're breaking up with me."

"I don't know what to say, Ronnie. I know you're lonely, and that you feel trapped, and that sucks. But..."

"When I've been at your house, no one seems to want things from you. You just...belong. It's a place where people go to simply be. You like each other. Maybe love each other, I don't know. I didn't feel lonely or trapped there. But your house is like a narcotic. Exhilarating but temporary. For me, it's a drug and I can't keep doing it. The day after, I could barely function, Mackenzie. Because no one was there. No one cared about me when I woke up."

"I cared," I said.

"I still owe you." She half smiled. "Take me there one more time? To your house?"

"You're engaged to another man," I said. "If I took you there, it'd be to extract something, and I don't want to do that."

She laughed, a bitter unhappy sound.

"How about your car then?" she said. "You can have me there. As an apology. I don't know what else to do."

I was sick and heartbroken, and not processing normally, and I almost said yes. I wanted her in every way a man can want a woman. I felt lonely, and being near the suddenly exposed gulf of misery that was Veronica Summers made it worse. Especially as she offered herself to me.

Mackenzie. Regroup. Think. Function. Talk.

"You contacted *me*," I said. "Not the other way round, after I left your bar."

"I know. It was foolish and spur-of-the-moment."

"Why did you?"

She rested her hands on her hips and bent at the waist, as though she'd run a race.

"I was lonely. And something about you felt complete. Whole, and comfortable. I wanted to be with a man who wasn't needy."

"And you don't anymore?" I asked.

"Mackenzie, please." Her voice cracked. "Don't do this. Let's just go to your car. That's how I can thank you. And apologize. It's the best I have."

"If I say yes, then we're through."

She sputtered, "We're through anyway."

The rain fell a little faster, hard drops that made her wince. Her shirt dotted like gunshot wounds.

"We're done for tonight. Maybe not forever," I said. "I don't want you for ten minutes only. If I say yes tonight, I'm no better than your fiancé. I'd take what I need and we'd go our separate ways. I don't want that."

"You want to be involved with an engaged woman?"

"No. I won't."

"Because of your principles," she scoffed. "Truth and honor and stuff."

"Yeah, sure, some of that. But also self-preservation. Because it'll hurt all parties too much. I've been down that road and it ends in a cliff. Why do it again? I need to be able to live with myself."

"Then what do you want?"

"I don't know. I don't know how this works." I shrugged, a stupid foolish gesture which meant nothing. "I don't know how life is supposed to be. I can't control anything, I'm just making this up as I go. Here's what I want - I want to be the kind of man who doesn't say yes to trysts from engaged women. That's all I got. I want to be the kind of man that you want to be with."

"That I want to be with?"

I nodded. "Correct."

"Life is hard, Mackenzie. None of us get what we want," she snapped. "The best we can do is say yes when small opportunities arise. Of course you're the kind of man I want to be with, but so what? I can forget you, that's what. For turning me down. No one turns me down, you sanctimonious, holier-than-thou...ugh, I don't know. I'm trying to be kind and pay my debt."

"I'm not turning you down. I'm saying, Not Like This."

"Whatever. I can't...I'm leaving. Goodbye, Mackenzie."

I had nothing to say, so I said that.

"And can you believe it? This is just the first of my secrets."

She darted into the road. Mercifully the light had only just turned green, giving her a small window to pass safely. I reached the edge but she was already on the other side and moving fast. Protected by the wall of traffic.

And then she was gone.

29

That night I kicked at sheets and threw pillows at Manny when he snored and I thought about Ronnie and her screwed-up life. At three in the morning I finally got up and drank three coffees to prop my eyes open.

Shucks, I thought. Ronnie's secrets were worse than I imagined. For the hundredth time, I told myself there'd been no way to guess.

This should be easy. I met a girl. Went on a few dates. Decided it won't work. Broke up. And now I move on. Done it before. I'll do it again, almost certainly. That's how this works.

It'll take time. The first night is the worst.

But.

The kitchen felt cold and empty, like a tomb. All my noises were magnified and hollow, like everything was vanity and temporary. Like I didn't matter.

But. But what?

But I liked the way this kitchen looked with her in it. I liked the back porch better when she stood on it. My bed was a better bed with her.

The stairs creaked. Manny softly treaded into the kitchen wearing socks, nodded blearily to me, and got a glass of water.

"Qué pasa, mi amigo."

"Nightmare," he said.

"What about?"

"Cleaning people off the street after a car crash."

"Ah yes," I said. "That's a fun one."

"You did a few of those?"

"I started out as Highway Patrol, remember?"

"What about you? Can't sleep?" he asked.

"I choose not to, because I am master of my fate."

"Oh shit."

"What?" I asked.

"Ronnie broke up with you."

"You don't know."

"Yes I do," Manny said.

"Yeah, she did."

He sat down with a coffee and drank it black.

"Why? Because you are ugly?"

"She's engaged," I said. "Told me tonight."

"Ouch. No es bueno."

"And I'm gorgeous."

Manny nodded and drank more.

"Sorry, amigo."

"I'm not sure about this one," I said. "Something's nagging at me. Telling me maybe I shouldn't quit."

"What do you mean?"

"The marriage was arranged by her father. And she's not happy about it. And, I don't know. I'm fond of her."

"You're fond? What, you are British royalty now? No one says fond."

"I mean it. Do I simply stop caring because she's with someone else? I'm into her. I knew she had baggage but...nothing about her has essentially changed. She's still the girl I want to see."

"She's getting married," Manny said.

"Maybe."

"You want her to have an affair? I know you, señor Mack, and you won't play the other man. Your heart is too...virtuous."

"Virtuous?"

"Yeah. Pretty good, right?"

"An excellent word. Language was invented for one purpose, Manny, and that is to woo women. And in that endeavor, laziness will not do."

"Gracias. I know all the good words," Manny said. "Are you quoting something?"

"I am. And. No, I don't want her to have an affair. I don't know what I want."

"You want to fix it. You're a fixer. You think you can fix everything. But some people? They are broken. And they can't be fixed."

"She doesn't want to marry him," I said.

"So?"

"So it gives me hope."

"Perhaps you are blinded by her appearance, jefe."

I shrugged and blew a blast of air at the ceiling.

"I don't know, Manny. Lotta pretty girls out there. But I want this one."

I couldn't explain it with words. And if I tried I'd sound immature and foolish, like a teenage kid. Because the truth was I felt bound to her. Drawn to her in ways I shouldn't be yet.

"You will have forgotten her by Friday," Manny said, and he went back to bed.

Perhaps. Perhaps not.

I stayed awake and got Kix up at six thirty and drank more coffee. Kix expressed concern over my caffeine intake. His babysitter, Roxanne, told me I looked sick and needed a day off.

I always hated Roxanne.

At school I noted Kevin was still missing. The semester wasn't half over and already he bordered on failing for absences. I had a terrifically witty comment about absences prepared for Megan but she was gone too. Her loss. Everyone gets days off but me.

I slept-walked through the day, and put movies on for the

students to watch so I wouldn't have to be smart. Jeriah asked if I was hungover. The Teacher of the Year committee might be having second thoughts, assuming they'd already voted for me. And I could think of no reason why they wouldn't.

At the end of the day I sat at my desk, feet propped and ankles crossed, and gazed absently out the window. Exhausted. One of those moments where we question who we are and why we're here and where we're going. And the universe responded with silence and kids making out in the parking lot.

I bet I looked like Ms. Bennett did at that moment. Deflated and tired. Just a couple of rookies, not yet good at life and feeling small.

In the hallway, Reginald Willis preached to no one in particular.

"It is a shame, I tell you, a shame. And I thank my lucky stars that my daughters are raised and gone, and that I didn't have to raise them in this violent age. Lord, Lord. With the rise of progress and wealth comes the corresponding perceived lack of wealth in less prosperous communities, and the despair and evil within. The second greatest trick the Devil ever pulled was convincing us that we're poor. And thus the violence. We can only pray that little girl is found, yessir, and it's a shame."

Something about the edge of his tone drew me out of my chair. I gathered belongings, locked my door, and met him in the hall.

"What's going on, Reginald?"

"I'm expounding on the evils of the world, of course, Mr. August."

"What girl are you referring to? The little girl who needs to be found?"

"I overheard Ms. Deere talking with the police," Mr. Willis said. "Little girl gone missing. Megan something or other."

"Megan Rowe? Little girl in glasses?"

"That's the one. Didn't come home last night and her parents are hysterical, for which I cannot blame them. You know her?"

His voice came from some distant place. Megan missing. Kevin absent. Silva's warning.

In my mind's eye, I was looking at Sheriff Stackhouse's photos of young girls kidnapped and murdered as a rite of passage. I was inside

Silva's truck and he was telling me of alternate ways he would wage war. Don't show up for work tomorrow, he said.

Megan Rowe.

I was her favorite teacher.

I started for the door. "I know her. She's in my first period."

"You know where she is?" he called.

I might.

I started picking up speed.

I HIT the 581 entrance ramp at seventy miles per hour. Traffic at three in the afternoon wasn't bad but some inconsiderate jerk dared to do the speed limit so I passed him on the ramp; my side-view mirror skimmed the guardrail and broke off.

I didn't know what was going on, but in my mind Silva was initiating a new recruit. Time for another rite of passage, which meant he needed a teenage girl. So he used his connections inside the school to acquire my class rosters and pick a girl. Megan Rowe.

I hoped I was guessing wrong. I hoped Megan ran away with her boyfriend or something, but dread settled over me like a blanket.

I dialed Sheriff Stackhouse.

"Pick up, pick up."

No answer. Voice mail.

Instead I shifted into fifth gear and maxed at ninety near Valley View. Thirty-five miles per hour over the limit. Thankfully the police displayed a shocking lack of vigilance.

I didn't know why I bothered paying taxes.

I didn't know anything. In the weeks I'd been at the school, I'd done zilch to help the cause. And signs pointed to the fact I'd made things worse. I'd kicked a hornets' nest and gotten other people hurt, and for nothing. No arrests. No new solid intel for the police. No gang generals. Only one missing teenage girl.

If she was dead then I'd have a hard time ever functioning again.

I called Stackhouse once more. No answer.

I knew only one way to help. Sheer stubbornness and sticking my neck out. So I skidded to a stop in the gravel lot off Shenandoah Avenue, at the collection of derelict brick warehouses.

Across the street, two trains rumbled noisily past. Rusty coal cars as far as I could see. Norfolk Southern pushing north, Union Pacific moving south.

This lot was where Eddie Backpack had gone in his gold Nissan. He said they unloaded trucks here. This was where I'd seen Big Will. And this was the only place I knew to look. I took my Kimber .45 and left the car door open, keys in the ignition. Chances were good I might need a quick egress, Big Will being the grumpy type.

I couldn't hear anything; the train generated too much sound.

I went around the brick building, an old car dealership office, and discovered the lot was larger than I'd assumed. Several acres deep. Old cars, stacks of tires, semi trucks, dump trucks, trailers, empty cargo bays, and warehouses stuffed with auto parts. And fresh tire tracks near the entrance.

This part of town felt vacant for miles, though I knew it wasn't. The place generated a forsaken vibe.

I didn't know what else to do, so I searched. First the two-story office building, which was empty except for roaches and wooden desks with expense reports from 1976. Nearby, two mammoth warehouses were stuffed with used alternators, hubcaps, Ford hoods and doors, rusted engines, oil cans, chains, but no little girls with tortoiseshell glasses.

So tired. Eyes burning. Every step I took sounded too loud. Wish I'd slept last night.

After an hour of searching, I struck pay dirt. Back corner of the lot. Three cars were parked at the chain-link fence, and one of them was a gold Nissan; the cars had been driven recently, but I saw no drivers. The adjacent structure looked like a receiving dock with four large cargo bays, doors pulled down. The gravel and dirt was worn by heavy tires leading to the bays. Muddy boot prints nearby. Muffled voices. Three of the bays were secured with heavy padlocks but not the closest bay to me.

Well. It was a good time to get shot.

I grabbed the heavy roll-up door and hauled. It rose upwards, well-oiled but loud, and slid to a stop along the ceiling.

Three men sat inside around a plastic table. At a glance, they appeared to be playing gin rummy. Hip-hop music issued softly from an iPhone speaker. One of the men was Eddie Backpack, wispy goatee and all.

Behind their small table was a waist-high wall of cocaine. A truly shocking amount, more than I'd ever seen in Los Angeles. Three feet high, five feet deep. Hundreds of white bricks wrapped with cellophane and duct tape. I was looking at ten million dollars minimum, and this was only the first cargo bay.

Two small monitors flickered in the corner. Security cameras. I'd been lucky they weren't paying attention. A scary-looking assault rifle sat propped against the wall.

I found myself in deep waters, far over my head.

"Hot dang," I said. "What's behind the other three doors?"

Wide eyes. Open mouths.

I brought my .45 up. I still had them in the throes of shock but it'd wear off.

Eddie Backpack said, "The fuck? Aren't you that teacher?"

"That's Mr. That Teacher, Eddie. Show some respect. Get those hands on the table, boys. You're in luck, because, believe it or not, I'm not after you. Nor your absurd mountain of illegal narcotics. That's... that is a lot of coke. Wow, do you guys ever lay down in the bricks and make cocaine angels? Do you mind if I do?"

One of Eddie's friends, a guy who looked a little like a roughneck Tiger Woods, said, "You're a dead white man."

"Probably." I thumbed the hammer back. "Tell me what I want to know and I'm going to close the door and leave. Sound good?"

No answers.

"I'm looking for a sophomore in high school. Her name is Megan Rowe. Wears glasses. I have a hunch your boy Nate Silva took her."

Once again, no answer. But I saw it in their eyes; they knew. They'd heard about the girl. My hunch was right—Silva had her, because of me. I felt rage and sorrow building up as pressure some-where inside.

I said, "What'll it be, kids? You took my favorite student. Shall I phone the police and we all wait till they arrive? Or you talk now and then run and I forget what you look like?"

Eddie Backpack's other friend, who did *not* look like Tiger Woods, went for his gun. A pistol in his pocket, which would require a full three seconds to retrieve. I took one step and threw a hard left into his jaw, where the bone connected under his earlobe. Something cracked, and it wasn't my hand. He slid off his chair and didn't move.

The assault rifle rested too far away for them to reach.

"Talk," I said. Silence. Eddie Backpack was showing greater forti-tude than during his encounter with Manny.

I fired my pistol into the cocaine bricks. The blast magnified in our enclosed space and my ears rang. Eddie and Tiger ducked and came up pale.

"Last chance," I said. Or at least I think I did. I couldn't hear myself.

Tiger's voice sounded as though he spoke underwater. "Listen, man. Calm down, okay? We don't got her."

"Who does?"

"Dunno."

"Not good enough." I stepped closer and leveled the barrel of my Kimber at Tiger Woods's knee.

"No! Shit, no, man, I dunno, Jesus. Eddie, you know?"

"Unh uh."

"Man, come on, point that someplace else."

I said, "You think you matter to me? You don't. And at the moment, neither does your cocaine. I can shoot you all day long without any guilt, because there's an innocent girl at stake. Is she alive?"

"I swear. I swear I don't know."

"Eddie, I'm shooting your friend in the knee. Watch carefully," I said. "Because you're next if you don't find a way to locate Megan Rowe."

"No, man! Shit no!" Tiger Woods spasmed and jerked his knees to the side, squirming away from the barrel.

I smiled grimly. "Hold still, kid. It's in your best interest. Else I'll shoot you in the crotch."

Tiger's knees were saved by their phones. All three phones sat on the table and they began beeping simultaneously. I saw the incoming texts.

>> **whos that**

>> **shoot that mother fucker**

>> **we coming**

I glanced upwards. Another security camera was bolted in the corner.

"I've been spotted," I noted intelligently. "Your salvation draws near."

"Like I told you. You a dead white man," Tiger said.

I hit Tiger in the nose. Blood spurted and Eddie flinched and stared.

"It's been a long day," I explained. "My girlfriend dumped me. So."

Eddie didn't say anything.

Like all brave heroes do, I fled. *We coming*, the phone said. Plural. And there was only little 'ol me. Live to fight another day. I was still in academia attire, which included topsiders, less than optimal for sprinting.

I reached the two-story brick office building and peeked around the corner. Just in time to witness my trusty Honda Accord being driven away, tires spitting gravel. There went my means of escape, at the hands of a hoodlum. Argh. He probably wouldn't treat her with the loving care she deserved.

Big Will had arrived. So had six of his friends. They wore jeans and red T-shirts, but Big Will wore the same hoodie I'd seen him wear before. Big guys, big arms. Perhaps what I found most daunting, however, was that each gentleman carried a shotgun. Every one of them, as though it was standard issue. It was like these guys thought ten million dollars' worth of cocaine was worth fighting for.

My heart, the coward, betrayed me and beat faster.

They came on. And I suspected more would arrive soon. How'd they get here so fast?

I inched away from the corner and ran for the fence. Thankfully the fence wasn't crowned with barbed wire or anything sinister. I summoned my youth and leapt higher than I had in years, got my hands on the top of the fence, and landed on the far side.

A cry raised behind me. Big Will and his merry men rounded the corner and witnessed my glorious leap. Big Will made eye contact with me. They were inside the fenced complex and I was out, standing on the circumventing sidewalk.

No sign of the trusty Honda. And I was a stranger in a strange land.

I bolted for the train tracks. Ran like a madman. I had to clear another fence, this one lower and constituted of chickenwire and old fence posts. I landed on the far side and a shotgun erupted nearby. Grains of shot tore into the fence post and tall grass and my shoulder.

Oooooouuuch.

"August!" Big Will called in that surprisingly high-pitched voice. "Get back here!"

"NO."

I stumbled and rolled down the embankment. Embarrassing. That never happened to Batman. I got to my feet on the gravel and ran south, parallel to the tracks. Big Will and at least three gunmen had come over the fence too.

The Norfolk Southern train was still there, but no longer in motion. Another shotgun fired, by the sound of it thirty feet back. The shot sparked against the steel alloy ahead of me. I slid between cars, climbed over the coupling, and moved deeper into the congested rail yard. One option was for me to stay there and shoot anyone emerging between the train cars but the odds weren't good. Running seemed the more sane choice.

This section of the railway yard was at least twenty lines deep, and therefore an ill-defined maze. I went over thirteen couplings and ran a half mile south before pausing to catch my breath. Distant

voices called to one another and locomotive wheels squealed somewhere in this world of steel. My shoulder muscles burned from the
metal pieces lodged within.

I found a rusty black car with a ladder and I climbed. The car was
empty and lined with coal dust. I let myself over and slid down inside.

I dialed the sheriff again.

"Pick up, Stackhouse," I panted.

But she didn't. Worthless public servant.

I waited for the beep. And then I told her voice mail, "Stackhouse,
there's a cocaine warehouse on Shenandoah, near 18th Street.
Millions worth of coke. If I get shot, and the chances are escalating,
then you should check it out pronto. Oh, and I think Nate Silva took
Megan Rowe."

I hung up.

I could call 911, but what kind of wuss does that? It'd be hard to
explain anyway. I needed to alert someone germane to the situation.

The voices grew near. The voices and the shotguns. It was impossible to accurately estimate the distance because of the metal sound
box I sat in, but they weren't far. I should have kept running.

I had a pistol, and I would be the better shot, but Big Will brought
at least three men with him and perhaps more. Bravery and idiocy
were not the same thing.

Suddenly, something happened. At first I couldn't tell what
because the entire world shook and moved.

The train I was on began churning. South, toward downtown.
Slowly at first, and all the couplings clanged as the distant locomotive
took their strain, but soon I moved at a brisk five miles per hour.

Hah. Saved by an engineer, unaware.

Still no return call from Stackhouse.

What about Sergeant Sanders? The Rottweiler-looking guy, big
forearms. Should have remembered him earlier, I had his number. I
rang him up.

"Sanders," he answered. Sounded like he was outside.

"Sanders, it's your friendly neighborhood drug hound. Got a hot
tip for you."

"Whaddaya got."

"You'll be happy to know I've been shot at."

"That does make me happy," he said. "Shame they missed."

"They didn't, not entirely. I went looking for Megan Rowe, the missing teenager from Patrick Henry, and I found Big Will's cocaine stash. And Sanders, it's a doozy."

"Oh yeah? Where at?"

I described it for him, as best I could without having the actual address.

"Make sure you go to the back corner. A loading dock with four doors. When last I was there, which was ten minutes ago, there were many shotgun-toting ne'er-do-wells," I said.

"On my way," he said. "Radioing for extra cars. Thanks Mack." He hung up.

I rode the train to freedom. With a small amount of satisfaction. But it's hard to be smug about one's accomplishment when sitting crisscross in a coal car, bleeding from the shoulder.

30

S tackhouse finally returned my call as I climbed down the car ladder and hopped off at Wachovia Tower. An October sun dropped toward the horizon and threw angry fall rays in my face. I scaled the fence and waited for her. Several hipsters walked by wearing suspenders, and they inspected me as though I was the funny-looking one.

Sheriff Stackhouse arrived. Her window was down and she said, "You look ridiculous."

"I am a fossil fuel. Where you been?"

"Problems out in Glenvar. Archery season. Guy shot his neighbor instead of a deer. Brush yourself off and get in."

I did. The resultant coal dust could have powered a city a few minutes.

She said, "Where's your car?"

"A mean guy took it."

"You let a mean guy take your car?"

"He was meaner than usual," I said. "Don't judge me."

"Sanders radioed. Told me he'd arrived on scene, following your lead. Maybe you should tell me the whole story."

"Good idea."

"My office. Over coffee. And we'll get a report from Sanders soon."

I rang Roxanne and told her I'd be late.

THE SHERIFF'S office connected to the city jail. A utilitarian establishment, not given to cheer or decoration. Amidst the dour-faced courthouse guards and receptionists and stern deputies, Stackhouse stuck out. Like I would at the Playboy Mansion, except exactly the opposite.

We went into her office and she fetched two Styrofoam cups of bad coffee.

"You look terrible," she said.

I coughed, and out came coal dust.

"And I'm not talking about the coal."

I said, "Didn't sleep much last night. And you should be nicer to your constituents."

"I don't need your vote. I won by a landslide."

"This coffee is not great, Stackhouse."

"Not why they hired me," she said. "Now. Tell me. All of it."

So I did. About spying Eddie Backpack on campus, trailing him to Cave Spring High School, finding Big Will at the decrepit lot off Shenandoah, being attacked at my home, Nate Silva's warnings, the Addisonian, Megan Rowe, the cocaine, and finally the shootings and train cars. She took notes on a legal pad, holding up her hand to slow me down occasionally.

"Manny Martinez help you with any of this?" she asked.

"Couple things."

"He's a good marshal. He bagged what's-his-name, Robin somebody, been on the run five months."

"Figured he be good. Taught him everything he knows."

She said, "You didn't mention your car."

"Big Will had it removed from the lot."

"An old Honda? License plate numbers?"

I told her, and she spoke into her radio and repeated the

numbers. Then she told me, "Doubt we'll find it. Lotta junkyards in that area, so it's probably already in pieces. But we'll look."

"Thanks."

She leaned back in her chair and blew a lungful of air at the ceiling. "The Megan Rowe girl is probably dead."

"I know. But I have hope. Or at least desperation. Have you heard of Big Will before?"

"He's in here about once a year. Failure to pay child support, drunk in public, assault, that kind of thing. Nate Silva has been squeaky clean, though. Could he be our guy?"

"The Bloods leader? Maybe. I dunno. Seems too unstable to run a big operation."

The door opened and Sanders walked in. Looking like a grumpy Rottweiler. It'd been an hour since I called him. He had on one of those long overcoats with the sleeves pushed up.

"So? Are we rich in cocaine?" Stackhouse asked.

"Got nothing. Zip."

I said, "Beg pardon?"

He dropped a set of Polaroids on the table. "This the place?" That was my loading dock and those were the doors. But the bays were empty. "Like I said, wise guy. Nothing."

Despite my professionalism and steely demeanor, I was stunned.

"What was I supposed to find?"

"A mountain of coke."

"Details," Stackhouse said. "I need details."

"Buncha kids in the lot when we pulled up and they scattered like rats. Someone had been there, that's for damn sure. Tire tracks and surveillance equipment. I called for the science guys to look at tracks and the electronics. I still got three cars there and a K-9 unit, searching. But right now? Bupkis."

"Nothing," I said.

"You got it, Mack."

He crossed his arms. Stackhouse stared out her window and seemed to lose some of the air which bolstered her posture. I did my best not to look sheepish.

"I got shot," I said. "So that's good."

"You're shot?"

"A little. Shotgun pellets in my shoulder. I'll swing by urgent care on the way home."

"You don't look so good, Mack. Maybe you dreamed this up?" he said.

"Sure, and then I shot myself in the back of my shoulder from long range with a shotgun."

"He didn't dream this up, Sergeant. We simply didn't get there quick enough," Stackhouse said. "Vice will open the investigation and maybe we'll get lucky. Mackenzie did his best."

"Best? Gave us nothing. Other than Big Will, who is a known commodity. The warehouse won't give us anything. We got zip."

"And Megan Rowe is still missing," I added helpfully.

"Who?"

"Missing teenage girl from Patrick Henry."

"Bah." He waved her away with a beefy hand. "She'll turn up. Probably ran away."

"Even so, I'm bringing Nate Silva in for questioning. He's in the back of a police car on his way here," she said. "Mackenzie, I've only just noticed the back of your shirt is caked with blood. I'll have you driven to urgent care and then back home. Sound good?"

"Sounds like a fitting way to end this day," I said. "Shrapnel extraction."

A DEPUTY DROVE me to the Lewis Gale emergency room, where a physician's assistant named Nick Floyd sewed me up and advised me not to get shot again. Solid counsel. I got home in time to eat a little dinner and put my son to bed. I read Kix a book and laid him in his crib. He held on to my finger and closed his eyes and drifted away.

The innocence of babes.

Dad lay on his bed watching Netflix, still wearing his tie and loafers. I waved and went for a beer.

Manny sat in a rocking chair on our front porch, drinking a beer and reading a Gabriel García Marquez novel, *Love in the Time of Cholera*. His bare feet were crossed and propped on the porch railing. I sat opposite and released a great weary sigh.

"That was a big sigh, amigo."

"It was intended to be great and weary, so you'll know how tired and important I am."

"I didn't get all that," Manny said. "I heard some excitement on the radio today. Sergeant Sanders. Was that you?"

"That was me."

"Is your mission complete?"

"It is not. I have possibly made it worse."

"What about Ronnie?" he asked.

"She has not called."

"You are having a bad twenty-four hours."

"Thank you, Manny. I noticed. You heard about the missing girl?"

"Sí."

"She was my student. I pissed off Nate Silva and he kidnapped her."

"You prove this?" he said.

"No. Not even circumstantial evidence."

"Wow. For this you are getting paid? Maybe you should give some of the money back."

"Already spent it."

"Want me to rough up Nate Silva?"

"Easier said than done," I said. "The police brought him in for questioning earlier. They won't find anything, he's too oily."

"You're going to do it yourself. I know you, señor."

"First, I'll get some sleep. I've been up thirty-eight hours. Tomorrow morning I'll find Silva's house and punch him in the mouth until he tells me what happened to her."

"You, jefe, are diplomatic and tactful."

"I don't know what else to do. So I'll try diplomacy until he bleeds."

Little Stevie our neighbor came sprinting down the sidewalk.

Probably it should be past his bedtime, but I guessed Stevie had very few boundaries set. It was certainly past mine. He leapt over the shrubs without breaking stride and cried, "They took him, they took him!" His eyes were wide, but they often were.

"Who took who, Stevie?"

"They came," he panted, standing on our stairs. "He didn't want to go but they took him."

"Your brother?"

"Yessir. Foster brother."

Manny placed a bookmark in his novel and set the book down. "Who took him?"

"His gang. He told them, he said he didn't want to be in the gang anymore. But they said he had to join. Tonight, Mr. August, and they took him. Just now."

"You think they'll hurt him?"

"Yessir I think. What do I do?"

"What do you want to do?"

"Get him back."

"Do you know where they went?"

"Maybe so. Kevin showed me once, said it was where they hung out." Stevie placed his hand on the railing and tried not to cry. His hand trembled. Poor little guy, sometimes life was simply too hard. I knew the feeling.

"Who is Kevin?" I asked.

"My foster brother."

My chest turned icy. Could it be? "Your brother a tall guy? Deep eyes? Get suspended from school recently?"

"Yessir that's Kevin."

I knew that Kevin. I shared a look with Manny. "Ah hah."

"What?"

"First of all, what are the odds? Kevin's the kid who tried to hit me in my first period. I'm surprised I've never seen him around the neighborhood."

"He don't go outside much," Stevie said.

"And second, they're going to make him kill Megan Rowe tonight.

No way it's a coincidence. They're in the same class, my class, and he has to join the gang the day after she goes missing."

Manny agreed. "Oh shit."

"Stevie, could you get me there? To the place he showed you?"

"I think so, maybe, Mr. August. It's near train tracks."

"Of course it is. Manny, I'd like to borrow your car. Mean guys stole mine."

STEVIE GOT ME CLOSE. Luck got me the remainder. We parked off Shenandoah on Baker, based on Stevie's hazy memory, and followed the sounds of locomotives. A private drive used exclusively for rail purposes was gated but not locked. I went through, down into what looked like a train car graveyard mud pit. An ill-kept dumping grounds for the industry.

I grew tired of trains.

The time was nearly ten and the sky must've been overcast because I saw neither moon nor stars. All looked dark. I proceeded without a flashlight, gun drawn.

Soon I began to hear the notes of human voices. Laughter and shouting. The noises led out of the mud and into a gravel supply lot, and I moved slowly, careful not to make noise or slip. Between two mountains of crushed stone I found them.

A girl lay unmoving on a filthy mattress. Had to be Megan. Silva's truck parked nearby, low beams illuminating the grisly party. Silva and Big Will each had a bottle in hand. Kevin stood nearby, awkwardly playing on his phone. Ugly Tiger Woods leaned against the grill of Silva's truck. Another guy sat crisscross near the mattress but I couldn't see him well.

"Waitin' on you, Kev," Silva said, putting the emphasis on "you."

Megan wasn't dead. And I'd arrived before Kevin did something he'd regret, but without time to spare. Could still salvage this nightmare.

Kevin mumbled something but didn't look up from his phone.

"What? Speak up, boy." Silva's biceps bulged against his black shirt as he took a drink.

"I ain't doing this."

"Oh yes you are. You dipshit, this is your party. Get on with it, I got work needs doing."

Kevin didn't speak.

"Put'cher phone away," Silva snapped. His bald head reflected light like the moon. "Or I'll break it."

Kevin complied.

"Been a long day, Kev. I picked this fine young thing out for you. Get on with it."

I got mixed signals from Big Will. He was an accomplice but perhaps an unhappy one. He didn't speak and his arms were crossed and his mouth twisted. At least he wasn't holding a shotgun.

I wanted to shoot them all from my hiding spot in the dark. Two problems, though.

First, I could kill one and maybe wound another before they found cover. But I'd still be outnumbered, and they'd call for backup immediately.

Second, I didn't shoot people in cold blood.

And also I was tired. So maybe three things.

I waited another couple minutes while Kevin stalled but he'd used up Silva's patience and he knew it. Things weren't getting better for him. Or for Megan. Or for me.

I thumbed the hammer back on the Kimber and left my hiding spot. If I die before I wake, I pray the Lord my soul to take.

They didn't see me until I stepped into their headlights. And the first thing they saw was light gleaming off my stainless steel gun, another reason to never buy blued metal.

"Hands where I can see them," I said. "You're nuts if you think I won't shoot you."

"Ho. Lee. Shee-yit," Silva said. "I can't even believe it. Look at this John Wayne *pinche gabacho* motherfucker."

I said, "John Wayne's a little dated. How about...Jason Bourne? Or John Wick?"

By design, Kevin was closest to me. I took one big step and hit him with my open hand. A big ringing slap, like being hit with a frying pan. Kevin fell and didn't get up. His friends yelped.

"Megan and I are leaving," I said.

"The hell is Megan?" asked Ugly Tiger Woods.

"Megan is the only girl here. Maybe I should use smaller words?"

Silva was squatting, eyes narrowed, and he looked like a coiled viper. A vein in his neck pulsed. "You ain't taking anyone." My gun hadn't left Silva but he seemed oblivious. Was I made of less stern stuff, I might have been concerned.

"Megan and I are leaving, Silva," I said, "even if that means stepping over your corpse."

Big Will was the true pro here. I knew it, he knew it, but maybe Silva didn't. Big Will took casual steps away from Silva, so I couldn't cover them both. There were too many guys here. My time ran short.

"Stop," I told Big Will.

He did.

"Hand it to you," Big Will said. "You stubborn, that's sure as shit."

Ugly Tiger Woods still had a busted nose from where I hit him earlier. He said, "Told you. Dead white man."

Now that I took another look, I recognized the last guy. I'd hit him in the jaw earlier today, when he'd gone for his gun. Busted Jaw didn't look happy to see me. In fact, very few of these guys did.

I had to shoot Silva. I needed their respect and their attention and Silva was the idiot in charge. Shoot Silva and get one of the guys to carry Megan out of here. No other way.

I took aim.

Big Will made a small motion. Small and innocuous. Not enough to startle me but enough to get my attention. He'd produced a gun from the pocket of his hoodie, a small .38 Special, and he pointed it at Megan.

"You decide, August. You fire, I fire," Big Will said.

I waited for a gunshot. A sudden burst of noise which would signal war. But none came. Cooler heads prevailing. The pressure built and abated.

"A stalemate," Silva said.

"Not for me," Big Will said. "I walk away. Told you this was stupid, Silva."

I said, "Fight you for her."

Silva blinked a moment. "What?"

"Round two, Silva. Me and you. Winner walks away. I win, I keep the girl."

He straightened and laughed. "You got it, *bolillo*. Beat yo ass." He tossed the bottle over his shoulder.

Big Will looked unsure. "Silva. August ain't a little dude."

"Fuck you, I got this."

Big Will nodded at my gun. "August. You putting that away?"

"I will. We got an agreement? Let us fight this out."

"I can trust you?"

"You should trust me more than you trust Silva," I said.

"I'll kill you, you don't keep your word. You get that?"

I pointed my gun at the ground and flicked the thumb safety. Slid the pistol back into its holster, and fastened it.

Big Will wanted to shoot me. Drill me now and be done with this. The debate crossed his face and stalled. Then, reluctantly, he put his pistol back into the hoodie pocket.

Silva took a knife from his ankle and came at me. He wasn't wasting time. I knew the knife; it was a KA-BAR. Used commonly in the American military. Seven-inch steel blade.

What a cheater.

He was going to cut me. A lot. Slash and dash and wait for blood loss to do its work. I'd been in a few back-alley knife fights in California, five hundred dollars to the winner. I knew how it worked. Open up enough veins and your opponent collapsed and you won. But usually both opponents had knives.

I knew a way to win the fight, and it wasn't pretty. Had to get close.

He slashed across his body and I let it pass. I stepped into him and presented my left shoulder, a big meaty target too big for him to ignore. It happened fast, he moved on instinct and stabbed into my side, just under my shoulder. The muscles parted and protested as the foreign object inserted itself into my body. The knife connected with rib bone.

But I was close enough and he was overly invested in his knife attack. Exposed. Vulnerable. I twisted, a short powerful rotation, and put an uppercut into his chin. Brutal impact. His jaw cracked. Teeth broke. Lights went out in his eyes.

He fell, pulling the knife out as he did, and landed in a twitching heap.

Thick hot blood poured freely down my left side. The cut was deep and wide, but I thought my lung was unscathed. I didn't have long, however, before I became weak.

Ugly Tiger Woods and Busted Jaw shouted and laughed. Enjoying the humiliation. Big Will did not. "That was quick," he said. He watched carefully to see if I went for my gun. I didn't.

I took off my button-up shirt and clamped it as best I could under my arm, over the wound, an inefficient bandage. I had a T-shirt on, but even shirtless I'd be unable to inspect the wound without a mirror.

Big Will was making up his mind on what to do when a car crested the rise above us and drove into the gravel supply lot. The blinding headlights threw us into sharp relief and I could see nothing past them. Two car doors opened. Marcus Morgan stepped into sight. Jeriah's father, tall and strong. His hands were on his hips and he glared at me, at Silva, at Kevin, both on the ground, at Big Will.

"The *hell* is going on?"

Ugly Tiger Woods had a pistol in his hands, twirling it on his finger like a gunslinger. "Better question is. Who you, old man?"

Marcus pointed at the mattress, the silver Tag on his wrist catching headlight. "Who's the girl?"

"Megan Rowe," I answered. "Silva took her."

"What happened to Kevin?"

"I hit him." My side was starting to throb and my head felt fuzzy. And I was confused. Why was Marcus here?

"Hit him. Why?"

"Best way to save his life."

"And Silva?"

Big Will answered, "The spic stabbed August. So August popped him good."

Much to my surprise, Sergeant Sanders stepped into the light. Pistol held loosely in his fist, coat pulled back to reveal the badge on his belt. "Everyone be nice and easy."

Marcus Morgan said, "Did I tell you? What did I tell you, Sanders?" He held his hands out, gesturing at the weird scene.

"You told me Silva was dangerous."

"I told you Silva was dangerous," Marcus said.

"To be fair," I said, "I told you that too. And also I'm confused."

"You. With the gun," Marcus Morgan said. Ugly Tiger Woods, the guy with the gun, paused. "Help Kevin into my car."

"Fuck you, old man."

Big Will took a deep breath and said, "Do it. Get the kid out of here."

Ugly Tiger Woods glared at Big Will.

"Do it. Now."

Tiger Woods and Busted Jaw hauled Kevin to his feet and helped him shuffle across the gravel, past the lights, and into the back of Marcus's car.

Sergeant Sanders, the big ugly Rottweiler, nodded at me. "You again. You're everywhere, Mack."

"Would you say I'm like Batman? Because I would."

"You're bleeding a lot, Batman."

"If you prick Batman, does he not bleed? How'd you find us?"

Sanders shrugged. "Following a lead. Marcus heard about tonight's initiation. What a got'damn mess." He walked to Silva and nudged him with a heavy boot. "You busted his face up bad, August."

"I think it looks better now."

"This idiot. Kept taking girls. Caused all our problems." Sanders aimed his gun at Silva's forehead and fired. The sound startled all of us. "Asshole caused enough trouble. More than he's worth."

Silva had been executed.

I was stunned. Only then did I notice the pistol Sanders held was a revolver. Not his police issue. Probably unregistered.

Whoa.

"You're in on this," I said. "On the whole cocaine operation."

Sergeant Sanders said, "Course I'm in on this. There's fuckin' millions to be made."

"Sheriff Stackhouse too?"

"Naw. Too schoolgirl. Goodie, goodie, a true believer, you know? About the only thing on her that ain't fake. And you didn't figure it, August, so maybe you ain't such a hotshot after all," Sergeant Sanders said.

"You got that right."

"I got that right."

Marcus Morgan crossed his arms and cast glances between us.

I realized, "That's how the drugs disappeared from the warehouse. I called you, Sanders, and you didn't radio for help. Not immediately. You took your time, gave them a chance to move the stuff."

"Hell, I helped them move it. I got a share in that stash. I make a bust that big, I get my name in the papers. Maybe a promotion. But I lose. I'm *this* close to packing up and moving to Argentina, you understand?"

"You told everyone about me. I couldn't figure out how my cover at school was blown so quickly. It was you."

Sanders grinned, a bad look on his twisted Rottweiler face. "You were screwed from the go, August. You're looking a little pale. Feel like shit, I bet."

"Let the girl go, Sanders."

"No can do. This doesn't end well for either of you."

Marcus, Big Will, Ugly Tiger Woods, and Busted Jaw had all been silent until now. Marcus stepped forward. "Wait. Sergeant, let's be cool about this. Mack is trying to do the right thing."

Sanders scoffed. "Marcus. Don't be stupid. He knows everything."

"I like August. Strikes me as a reasonable man."

"Reasonable as heck," I agreed.

Marcus indicated me with a nod. "He knows the big picture. Doesn't mind breaking rules."

"Oh yeah, tough guy? You won't tell anyone?" Sanders asked.

"Oh, not that reasonable," I said. "I'll throw you straight in jail."

Marcus grunted. I disappointed him.

"Let the girl go," I said again.

"No."

Marcus said, "Sergeant, the girl's done nothing."

"She's seen faces."

"So? She can't identify anyone. She was drugged, and her captors all look the same."

"All look the same?" Sanders said. "That like a racist comment 'cause you guys are black? Hell, she's black too."

Marcus took a deep, patient breath. "Not because we're black. Because it was dark and she's been drugged."

"Listen. Marcus. Appreciate the help. I do. But shut the fuck up. You're over your head. Big Will, we're going to move some gravel. Find us something to do it, eh? And you two." He pointed a thick finger at the two kids, looking a little confused. "I don't know your names..."

"I call them Ugly Tiger Woods and Busted Jaw," I offered.

"Whatever. Ace August here and move the bodies to that gravel pile. At least he'll stop running his mouth."

Marcus shook his head, a little movement Sanders didn't see. The men hesitated.

Big Will cocked an eyebrow, looking between Sanders and Marcus. He hadn't gone for the gravel mover.

This was going downhill. Fast. I still had a gun in my holster, but I was feeling woozy. Fingertips numb. Blood had reached my shoes.

Sanders threw up his hands, waving the gun. "You don't hear so good? Waste August and get me a gravel mover."

Again, Marcus Morgan gave his head a small shake—no.

Big Will stood still.

But Ugly Tiger Woods and Busted Jaw decided they'd play along.

Apparently they respected Sergeant Sanders more than Marcus Morgan. And they owed me.

"Dead white man." Ugly Tiger raised his pistol and began squeezing.

"Safety's on," I lied.

He paused.

Marcus snapped, "Put down the damn gun."

I slid to the right and grabbed Tiger's hand. I bent the gun backwards until he yowled. The gun fired and missed, making my head ring. Busted Jaw tried for a shot but I pivoted away. Tiger couldn't shake loose, his wrist about to break. I elbowed him in the nose and the gun released. Into my hands. I was weak, muscles moving without much conviction. Like operating from a distance. I got the gun barrel under his chin and I pulled the trigger. A sick muffled crack, and Tiger Woods's face went slack and he slumped against me.

Busted Jaw maneuvered for a shot and he fired. Missed, shooting Tiger's shoulder instead. I slid from under Tiger and shot Busted Jaw in the forehead. His head kicked back and he collapsed.

So weak. Hard to move.

Big Will smacked my hand and the gun clattered among the stones.

There was blood on both my hands. Couldn't get enough breath.

Marcus Morgan threw back his head and laughed, standing a little taller. "Damn, Mack! Here I was, thinking you're a Christian."

"Just not good at it yet."

"You see this, Marcus?" Sergeant Sanders had his gun on me. "Look at this mess. This is why we do things *my* way. Get it? Now we got two more dead bodies. Got'damn it."

A radio squawked underneath Sander's overcoat. Something about reports of shots fired off Shenandoah.

He spoke into it. "This is Sergeant Sanders. I'm already over here. Looks like kids playing pranks with fireworks. Disregard."

Marcus clasped his hands behind his back and said, "Hold up, Sergeant. Think about it. Mackenzie didn't call the police. I respect that about him. Came here to handle it himself. A lot about this man I respect."

"In hindsight," I said, "probably would have been wise to call."

"Christ, why are we talking?" Sanders said. "I'll shoot him myself." He raised his revolver again.

Marcus Morgan brought his hands around. His right hand now held a Glock. He fired into the back of Sergeant Sanders's head. I flinched at the noise. Sanders slumped onto the ground awkwardly and Marcus shot him twice more. The sounds and flashes froze the moment in time. Indelibly burnt into my eyes.

Marcus said, "You outlived your usefulness, Sergeant."

"Lucky he called off the radio," Big Will grunted, looking calm despite the violence. "Gives us time."

Marcus and Big Will and I watched each other. The last men standing. Surrounded by four dead bodies, and Megan Rowe.

"If I wasn't on the verge of unconsciousness," I said, "then I would be really surprised. Instead I just feel like I'm flying."

"Will, we need a cleanup," Marcus said.

"Yes sir." Big Will walked to the car and opened the trunk.

"You just shot a cop," I said. Marcus nodded. "And you're an Episcopal."

"Trying to be," Marcus said. "Like you, I'm a work in progress. You and me, August, we're alike."

"It's you. You're the General," I said.

"That's an arcane term, and you know it. I'm a damn businessman."

"I was hired to find you."

"Here I am. Told you, in high school, I hustled. Delivered papers. Did what I had to do. Hard work."

Big Will came back with two trash bags. He removed my Kimber from its holster and handed it to Marcus. Marcus pushed on the safety, checked the chamber, and shoved it into his belt. He tossed his Glock into the trash bag. Big Will knelt beside Silva's body and rifled through his pockets.

"You're a business man?" I said.

"That is correct."

"You're running the show. The cocaine."

He shrugged. "I'm in many businesses, and cocaine is one of them. I control the traffic in all directions for two hundred miles. But I'm not *in* a gang; I hire them."

"And Silva was...?"

"For hire. And a headache. Uncontrollable agency, pissing me off. Bad for business. He came here from California and brought all the unnecessary hate. Too wrapped up in the thug life. He started killing girls for no reason."

Big Will collected Silva's knife and gun and wallet and phone, and he moved to Ugly Tiger.

My head swam. Stackhouse thought Silva and Marcus were the same person, a violent heavy hitter recently moved from California nicknamed the General. But Silva was violent and new, and Marcus the true heavy hitter. Two persons, not one.

"Let the girl go, Marcus."

Marcus nodded and walked to the mattress. His shiny black shoes looked out of place in the blood and rubble. "I plan to. Silva thought these juvenile rites of passage were important."

"You don't?"

"I don't. Do you know what gangs are, August? They're kids. Broke adolescent alcoholics. I don't even speak to them, usually. I send liaisons, like Big Will."

"They're also people. People with families and priorities and dreams." My "s" sounds were coming out slurred, and I had a funny taste in my mouth.

"Makes them easier to exploit, August. They are adolescents in need of identity and purpose. The gangs give them that, and then I give the gangs money and work. I have a degree in accounting from Princeton, you understand. I turned down offers from the fucking FBI and Wall Street. I bring peace and order to the drug trade. It would be so much worse without me."

"Big Will called you tonight," I said. "He told you Silva had another girl. You and Sanders came to kill Silva."

"As I said, I limit the violence when I can. Do you realize how big this is, August? Silva didn't. I have cops in my pocket. I got FBI too. I'm moving tens of millions every month. I snap my fingers and a hundred guys show up. The gangs are mercenaries. Local hired militia for grunt work, that's all."

"You get tax breaks for that?"

Big Will crouched next to Sergeant Sanders's body. He took two phones and two guns off him.

Marcus said, "I like you, Mack. My son, he likes you too. You been good to him. So we are at an impasse, but we got something working in our favor."

"Good looks?"

"Call it mutual respect. You and I, let's live and let live. That's the best deal you'll ever get."

My stomach lurched from the light-headed dizziness. I bent over and dry heaved. Embarrassing.

He said, "You need stitches. I'll drive, to the hospital."

"Do you tithe off your drug money?" I wiped my mouth with my sleeve.

"You're being blithe."

"I'm being hilarious."

"Plan on telling the sheriff?" he asked.

"Probably."

Big Will stopped his collection and glanced at Marcus, and shook his head.

Marcus said, "Mack. I got ten eyewitnesses put me somewhere else. Plus I got preset digital alibis. You can't win, it won't work."

He returned to his car and came back with an emergency first aid kit. He lifted up my T-shirt and opened the kit.

"I saved your life, Mack. Tonight, and other nights. Silva wanted your ass. Sergeants Sanders talked about killing you multiple times. So did Big Will. But my boy, Jeriah, he said you're a good man."

"That's very nice." I winced. "I'll bring you cookies in prison."

"And I'm trying to save you once more. Big Will, he's gonna shoot you, you realize. Don't be a fucking moralist. Hold this bandage tight. It's covered with disinfectant cream."

I did. The world was dimming.

He said, "Think about it. I arranged for Roanoke's most violent criminal to be killed tonight. And I shot a corrupt cop. I got Roanoke's best interest at heart. That, and money."

"Two wrongs making a right? That your argument?"

"This is our city. Mine and yours. It's a good place. I keep the wolves at bay. Believe that, August, it could be worse. A lot worse. You try to take me out, trust me, it gets bad."

He had a point there. I'd encountered a lot of mobsters. Marcus seemed the brightest and sanest of the bunch. On the other hand, I might be going into shock and not thinking clearly.

He said, "I didn't let them come to your house, Mack. I'mma keep you alive, this one more time. We'll attend church together. Dinner with our families. Talk about raising boys."

My words were mixing. "I can't jus' pretend, Marcus. Preten' we're friends, this did'n happen."

"Do you think you can stop the drugs? Never. They'll hand the operation to someone like Silva. See. I'm not stupid. I know your Mexican friend is hidden nearby, gun trained on me. I bet he's almost shot Big Will and myself a dozen times tonight. It'll be a race between me and him. Or Big Will and him. See who hits their target first."

Big Will carried his bag of stuff to the car and closed the hood. "Marcus. Man, we need to go. Want me to ace the asshole or what?"

My Kimber was in Marcus's hands. He took out a rag and wiped it down, and then held it in the rag. "The marshal's out there, Will. You try and we're dead men."

Big Will turned in a circle, inspecting the dark. "You think? Why he ain't shot yet?"

"My guess, he trusts August to handle it himself. Plus, August told him not to, except in the fucking direst of emergencies. I respect that." Marcus took a deep breath and looked at the mattress again. Back at me. "Consider your beautiful son, Mack. And my boy Jeriah. They don't need to be orphans. If I die? Or end up in jail? They'll come looking, Mack. The big swinging dicks in Washington, the Kings. In Miami, New York, Atlanta, they won't let the cocaine stop. They'll look for my killer and they'll find you. They'll kill you and Kix and your father. Promise you that. You understand that I ain't threatening your son. It's just gravity. That's how things will fall out if the others get involved."

I wavered on my feet.

He said, "I did my research. I know you killed a man last year to protect your son. You should consider letting a man live now for the same reason. You don't, I promise your boy will be fitted for a small coffin. And lowered in the ground next to you. The people I work with? Nightmares. They didn't go to Princeton. They'll kill my boy too."

He pressed the pistol into my hand. I couldn't grip it.

"You and me," I managed to say, "Aren't. Finished."

"I want you alive, August. I don't say that to many people."

He turned and walked back to his car.

I fell to my knees and then my face.

31

Manny drove to the hospital. I was conscious but not entirely in my right mind. The world was cold. Megan Rowe lay in the backseat of his car with Stevie. What a mottled crew.

The towel I lay on kept shifting, and Manny complained about the leather and he poured old Pepsi into my mouth.

"Drink the sugar, amigo. Keep you out of shock."

I grunted, "You ever gonna shoot anyone? Why didn't you shoot Silva?"

"You had it covered, señor Mackenzie. Never a doubt."

"He stabbed me."

Manny said, "Yes, I felt guilty about that."

"Coulda called...called for backup."

"Could. But I got caught up in the fun. I can kill Marcus Morgan anytime I want. Besides, you wouldn't want me to shoot Silva. You wanted him for yourself."

"What I want. Is for you. To shoot somebody."

"Next time." He grinned.

"Going to...throw up again."

We made it to the hospital before I did.

~

NICK FLOYD, the physician's assistant, thought I was hilarious. "Well," he said, "I told you not to get shot again. And you didn't; you got stabbed. I'll be in tomorrow at seven, in case you get burned or poisoned."

He gave me a transfusion and sewed me up.

A couple hours later I felt much better, thanks to blood and morphine and Zofran. I could sit up without vomiting. Small victories.

Attorney Adam Moseley, Stevie's guardian ad litem, came to pick him up and take him home. Big guy, big Navy voice. He took one look at me and said, "You need a lawyer, call me."

"But what if I need a good one?"

"I'm the best there is, asshat." He left, Stevie in tow.

Manny said, "I like Counselor Moseley."

Manny was brought more juice and food than I was by the nurses. He probably could score Dilaudid if he asked. He read his novel, feet crossed and propped on my bed. He didn't get up when Sheriff Stackhouse came into my small corner of the emergency room.

"Mackenzie," Stackhouse said. She had on jeans, boots, and a tight sheriff's office windbreaker. "You've had a hell of a day."

"I am aware of this."

"I just left Megan Rowe's room. She essentially spent the last twenty-four hours on a forced cocaine bender, but should recover. Her parents are beside themselves. Where'd you find her?"

I said, "Gravel supply lot, near a train car dumping ground. Nate Silva took her."

"Where's Silva now?"

"You'll find him there. Along with a few others."

Manny whistled tunelessly and turned a page.

"You shot him?" she asked.

"No. I'm an Episcopal. I only shot his friends."

"Oh hell."

"I'm not a very good Episcopal. I skipped last week."

She said, "Who killed Silva? No wait, I need to write this down. And I don't know where the hell Sanders went, he's not returning my calls."

"Stackhouse," I said, and she stopped searching for paper and a pen. "Listen to what I say first, and then decide if you want to write it down. Trust me."

"Okay. Go."

I told her Silva kidnapped Megan Rowe to make me stop poking into his business, and about how I'd found their execution spot thanks to my neighbor. I told her Silva had been the one kidnapping girls, and he'd arrived from California last year. I told her about the fight and Silva's knife and Sanders driving up and shooting Silva. She held up her hand and said, "Sanders? Shot Silva?"

"Worse than that. Sanders was working with them. For years, I surmise."

A long pause.

"That can't be true," she said.

"I can prove it. Couple hours ago, he called off reports of gunfire. Said it was kids playing with fireworks. But it wasn't. It was his gun."

"Sanders is helping move cocaine," she said, kind of on autopilot.

"Was. Yes."

"Was," she repeated.

I nodded. "He's beside Silva, at the gravel supply lot."

She sat down on my bed. On my foot. "Dead."

"Shot three times by one of the drug traffickers who thought he'd grown too headstrong."

Manny looked at me curiously and went back to whistling.

"What will I tell his wife?" she said, hollow and distant.

"You could tell her the truth. Nate Silva, a local leader of the Bloods, is dead. He moved a lot of cocaine. And Sanders shot him. Tell her that. It's the truth."

"Part of the truth. But not all."

I gave her a few more details, but so far I hadn't mentioned Marcus Morgan. His words had struck me. Hard. I had a vision of Kix's coffin being lowered into the ground. His broken little body inside, and I about came undone. I'd go to any extent to keep that from happening, and Morgan was right; gang cartels were notorious for going after families.

Plus, Marcus saved my life. Multiple times, from the sound of it.

Marcus Morgan and I weren't done. He still had to deal with me. But I wasn't ready to risk the police yet.

Stackhouse turned to search my face with that nasty piercing glare detectives develop over time. "Stuff you aren't telling me?"

"Yes ma'am, there is. Haven't decided about it yet."

"Why?"

"If I tell you, it might make Roanoke a less safer place. For me, for you, and for my son. And I've told you the truth. Just not all of it. It's up to us to decide if Sanders is a hero or not, so to speak."

She said, "I don't know you well enough to trust your discretion, Mackenzie. I'd prefer not to bring you in on withholding evidence and obstruction of justice charges."

"You got the violent criminal you were after. And my investigation isn't done yet. You'd only muddy the waters."

She twisted to inspect Manny, who innocently read his book. Then back to me. "You two dumbasses are a handful. You know that. I don't care how pretty you are."

"Can you tell Ms. Deere that I won't be in tomorrow? She scares me," I said.

"No. I have dead bodies to examine. Don't be a wimp, kid."

The curtain pushed aside and my father stepped through. Kix was in his car seat carrier, leaned back and sleeping. Dad was holding the carrier like a bag of groceries.

"I got the phone call all fathers long to get," Timothy August said. "My boy has been stabbed. How are you, son?"

Kix shifted positions and sighed in his sleep.

"I've been stabbed. Lesser men would complain."

"Manny, how could you let him get stabbed?"

Manny shrugged. "Ask me, it's a miracle it doesn't happen more often, Señor August."

Dad didn't listen. His attention had already shifted to Sheriff Stackhouse. "Why hello there."

"Timothy."

"How about that dinner you owe me?" he asked.

"Always the charmer, aren't you. Turning into quite the silver fox."

"And you," he said. "Gravity seems to have no effect."

Manny made an amused noise that no one heard but me.

"No dinner. We should catch up over a cocktail," Stackhouse said.

"I would like that above all things."

They were standing far too close for people who barely knew each other.

She said, "Not tonight. My evening just got booked solid and I have to go kick ass. Tomorrow?"

"It's a date."

"Gross," I said. "What the heck just happened."

32

A week later, I read about Sanders' funeral in the paper. As a fallen officer, he'd been given a special procession and service. The mystifying events at the gravel supply lot were hard to figure, but one thing was for certain: Sergeant Sanders died in the line of duty and took down a major criminal with him. What a hero.

His longtime friend Marcus Morgan delivered the eulogy, which I read with mild amusement and disgust. I wasn't sure what to think of Marcus. He'd spared me—several times over. That counted for something. Good taste, for one thing.

I sat in my office and stared blankly out the windows. I had a list of attorneys to call, all of whom were screaming for my services. Good help is hard to find, and all that. I'd taken a week off from teaching to recover, but was scheduled to return tomorrow. Couldn't decide which career path I'd rather travel, teaching or investigation. Two roads diverged in a yellow wood and I was too blah to choose. And the stitches under my shoulder hurt.

My stairs creaked and groaned softly. Could it be? Princess in distress? The door was open and a woman I didn't know stuck her head in.

"Mr. August?"

"Yes, come in."

She was fifty-five, red hair cut in a stylish bob, professional pantsuit, black handbag. "Do you have a moment?"

"I have plenty of moments."

"I've never talked to a private detective before."

"I'm not sure I have either," I said. "Not many of us around. Please sit."

"How were you injured?" She indicated my arm, which was in a sling for another day or two.

"Walrus."

She sat. "I need help."

I nodded.

"It's a matter of...desperate delicacy. And I was told you could be trusted. Can you?"

"I can be. Who directed you my way?"

"My attorney. And, in a funny coincidence, my favorite bartender. A Miss Veronica Summers. Do you know her?"

"I do." My chest tightened a little. I'd been trying not to think about Ronnie, and I'd been failing. A lot. "She's my favorite bartender too."

"She gave you the highest praise. I thought it was too cute. She said she'd never met a man of integrity before she met you. All others, she said, pale in comparison. Isn't that darling?"

"It is. But perhaps she's merely spent her life with awful men."

"It's possible. She seems quite fond of you. Which reminds me." She opened her black handbag and withdrew an envelope. "She requested I deliver a card."

The envelope had my name on the front. The word "Mackenzie" never looked so good. I opened the seal and withdrew a handwritten note.

MACKENZIE,

I am a mess.

I know our romance was brief.
And ill-fated from the beginning.
But I'm having trouble moving on.
Please think of me often?
I find my life more bearable...
if I can believe you haven't forgotten me.
- Ronnie

I READ it twice and returned the note to its envelope.

She said, "Mr. August, it must have been a good note. You look so happy."

"That's because it's a beautiful day. What a time to be alive. How can I help you?"

THE END

❧

Dear reader, I hope you enjoyed August Origins (You did). I have two suggestions for your next book.

The first suggestion is The Desecration of All Saints, released in October, 2019. It's a Mackenzie August mystery that takes place very soon after the novel you just finished. It is not Book 2 of the Mackenzie series. Think of it as Book 1.5. Mackenzie is hired to investigate the most powerful man in his city—the priest. Click here.

My second suggestion is Book 2 of the series, called The Second Secret. Click here.

You'll enjoy either one (almost certainly).

FROM THE AUTHOR

Clearly I've been influenced by the greats.
Raymond Chandler.
Mickey Spillane
Robert Parker
Sue Grafton
Too many to mention them all.
It occurs to me that several of my favorites died recently, so now I'm worried about Robert Crais and Janet Evanovich.

I am an independent author and need your help to continue my writing career. Word-of-mouth and Amazon reviews are the two things keeping writers like me in business. If you enjoyed the book, your feedback would go a long way. Many many thanks in advance.

Thanks to Adam, Stephanie Parent, Sarah, Jackson, Chase, and everyone else who makes life worth living (which includes iced vanilla coffees and Mill Mountain Coffee's omelettes.)

You can get book two here- Second Secret
Mack runs into an ex-girlfriend from college.

Ronnie needs help with her second secret.
Mack gets pulled into the criminal underworld.
(It's really good.)
(Obviously.)

If you enjoy book two (and you will), I'll send you the Mackenzie August prequel *The Last Teacher* for free when you finish.

Excerpt from Book Two, *The Second Secret*

The skies were clear and business was booming.

Except I didn't want to do any of it. I needed a day off from photographing romantic trysts and searching for missing teenage runaways. So I did what all trusty and industrious private detectives do in their downtime; I searched online for new grill recipes, and practiced drawing my gun from the holster, Wild West style.

Fortunately for me, and also for the client, I was sitting down at my desk when the stairs creaked. Someone knocked softly on the door and entered.

A blonde. She wore a white blouse and one of those skirts which is already too short and then has a professional slit running halfway up the side. Heels and a tan, no hose.

She was perhaps the prettiest person I'd ever seen in real life.

"Hello, Ronnie," I said.

"I'm in need of a professional private detective," she said. "Are you accepting clients?"

"I'm your man."

The air in the room was hot and electric. She inspected me. I watched her inspecting me. Both of us flushed a little. I almost flinched each time our eyes connected.

"I'm serious, Mackenzie. This is a professional call."

"Then you should put on an overcoat."

"But how would you look at my legs?"

"I have a degree in criminal investigation. I'll find a way," I said. "Close the door behind you."

"If you're accepting clients, and you think we can work together, I'll go fetch him."

"Fetch who?"

"The client," she said. "My father."

Made in the USA
Middletown, DE
22 November 2020